# REDEMPTION
# ISLAND

## ISLAND DUET ONE

# L.B. DUNBAR

L.B. Dunbar
Redemption Island

Copyright © 2017 Laura Dunbar

Cover Design: Shannon Passmore/Shanoff Formats
Cover Image: Stocksy
Edits: Kiezha Smith Ferrell/Librum Artis Editorial Services

# Other Books by L.B. Dunbar

## The Sensations Collection
*Sound Advice*
*Taste Test*
*Fragrance Free*
*Touch Screen*
*Sight Words*

## The Legendary Rock Star Series
*The Legend of Arturo King*
*The Story of Lansing Lotte*
*The Quest of Perkins Vale*
*The Truth of Tristan Lyons*

## Paradise Stories
*Paradise Tempted: The Beginning*
*Paradise Fought: Abel*
*Paradise Found: Cain*

## Stand Alones

*The Sex Education of M.E.*

*The History in Us*

## The Island Duet
*Redemption Island*
*Return to the Island*

## Modern Descendants – writing as elda lore
*Hades*
*Solis*
*Heph*

Redemption Island

# Inspiration

"If you succeed in judging yourself rightly, then you are indeed a man of true wisdom."

- Antoine de Saint-Exupéry, *The Little Prince*

Redemption Island

# Prologue
## *The Island Sees You*

Terrence Jackson Corbin IV understood right from wrong. He'd been doing right his whole life, until one day he chose wrongly. He didn't know why he did it, only that he did. He wanted to be something other than who he was. For one night, he wanted reckless and meaningless and bad. But sometimes bad goes too far, and he had pushed that limit. He'd crossed it actually, and the result faced him.

Tack, the name he took for himself, stared at the island over the bow of the racing boat. Secluded, lush, and bursting with greenery, the sensuous curve of the natural landscape ahead seduced him. He'd spend one year in this place—alone. He longed for the solitude. His world had grown too chaotic, and he'd take this penance. Banishment. Reflection. However, the board wanted to dress this up, it was what it was—punishment. He had to face the consequences of his crime, and an alternative process of justice was provided. Father had friends in high places.

Jail time in the family story wasn't an option for the opulent Corbin family. No, the token son—the only son, the single, blessed child—could not face such a heinous mark on his resume, despite the cruelty of his crime.

*A year off*, his mother muttered through the over-Botoxed, pinched smile forcibly plastered on her pristine face. She'd never look at him the same again. She'd never forgive him in the name of womanhood, but her devotion to her husband and the wealth of his income kept her silent to her true feelings.

*A year to discover what's important*, his father sternly emphasized, narrowing his green eyes, the same eyes that graced his own face. His father believed a year without modern conveniences and frivolous amenities would remind Tack of the privilege he had. It would also remind him that his father had the power to heartlessly squash him like an annoying insect.

*A year of reflection,* the softly spoken restoration coach had interjected. Tack thanked the heavens and lucky stars for the intervention of his father's lawyers and their assistants to find an alternative to prison. Tack could admit he'd never survive becoming the bitch to another man. His pampered life emanated from his pores, and he sensed that a sex-starved inmate could smell his weakness a mile down a dusty road. On the other hand, no one understood the injustice Tack had already endured. He'd learned to fight back, but more often with words than his fists. It wouldn't help him in an eight-by-six cement room with a metal cage for a door.

The island drew closer as the bow cut through the Caribbean waters. Tack smiled to himself, inhaling the allure of a tropical paradise before him. He'd been warned. There was no resort here. No swimming pool or weight room. No daily spa or five-course meal. No unlimited bar. This would be only Tack and nature. He laughed. He didn't need those glorified amenities. He needed to be alone. He wanted to get away. A year on an island by himself sounded heavenly. Five-star accommodations or not, this punishment would be a piece of cake.

++

Juliet Montmore had nothing left. Everything had been stripped from her on that fateful night. A crime committed against her, so heinous, so vile, nothing remained of who she was or who she wanted to be. The little she had before, the short distance she'd come, all disappeared that night. Innocent, curious, unsuspecting, she'd followed like the lost sheep she once had been. But she was no longer easily tamed. Her inner wolf sprung free. Her crime had been justified for the one done to her.

She stared forward as the bite of ocean spray nipped at her face. She closed her eyes with the sense of freedom. Three months in a detention center had done things to her. It built her strength. It restored her desire. She'd never be taken advantage of again. The thought held her head higher. She refused to wobble with the bounce of the metal craft over reckless water. Her good behavior had paid off.

*A one year experiment,* her mentor offered her as compensation for her detainment. Time was needed to prove the justification of her release. The social worker for women's rights wanted to prove Juliet hadn't displeased any god. A man had done what he'd done to Juliet. Her response was warranted. His life for hers.

*A year to repent,* her uncle suggested, shaking his greasy-haired head and lowering his eyes. The solicitous gaze under those lids hinted that she'd deserved what happened and expressed his sorrow that he hadn't been the one to think of it. Or perhaps, he had, only he didn't act on his fantasy. Tormented her, yes, but acted, never. How sorry he'd have been if he had, as her actions had proved.

*A year to restore,* the masculine voice of the Native American liaison interjected. Rich in cultural heritage, the concept of circle justice had reached a modern age of restoration for sins. Whatever one does to another has to be rectified to find inner peace. Juliet did want that peace, so the concept of being alone appeased her. Her thoughts haunted her, but the idea of being away from her limited family, people who were no longer willing to be her friend, and the dreams she had lost, sounded appealing. A year on an island—alone—sounded heavenly.

The engine cut, the speed lowered, and the metal skiff drew forward into a small bay surrounded by an alcove of trees hovering over the water's edge. The sudden fragrance of sweet fruit and salt air was intoxicating. Juliet did not fear the lack of modern amenities. She'd been raised on scraps, provided with little clothing, and discouraged of her dreams. She was a survivor. She could hunt and trap, fish and find berries. A small shelter was provided for her protection from the elements and the concept of having her own place, a space to be free, seemed like a fantasy. Repentant for sin or not, this tropical haven was the religious revival she needed. She'd atone in the sun, bask in freedom, and hold no regret for the evil she'd done.

# 1

# Day 1 - Tack

After the motor boat sped away, I stood surrounded by four giant trunks. I had every survival item imaginable for a luxurious camping trip, but all I wanted was to find the hammock designed to hang from trees. I wasn't going to waste a moment of my paradise banishment. Wiggling my bare toes in the sand was step one. A nap in the shady heat would be my second act.

The only information I had about this place was its isolation and reported safety, meaning, it was relatively free of inhabitants other than monkeys, birds, and some giant-sized insects. I didn't worry about food, as provisions were promised to be delivered, and a botanical guide had been provided to help me decipher plant life. My father thought living below my means would be an excellent lesson in humility. I scoffed at the thought. *What did he know about being humble?*

"There are people less fortunate than you, Tack. You're wasting what's been provided for you." The statement sounded callous and clinical, not surprising from an unfeeling man who lacked emotion. He knew nothing about tenderness. Born the first son to a prominent family, tracing their history back to the original settlers of America, pride ran deep in the blue blood within our family's veins. My father was the poster child of privilege generating prosperity. Only he didn't follow the common philosophy of those well-off to be generous. My father hoarded his dollars, dispensing funds with a calculated purpose. He often commented that I wasted his hard-earned money.

I laughed again at the thought. My father's money came from money before him and would exist long after me if I didn't squander it like my father warned. Terrence Jackson Corbin III was full of cautionary advice for his son, Terrence Jackson Corbin IV. His biggest suggestion: *Don't get caught.* So when I did, the expense was more a disappointment than the crime committed.

As to that crime, billionaire Terror Corbin, as he was known among the industrial elite, didn't even blink at the accusation. What was the taking of a woman against her will to him? Certainly not the legally termed word—rape. No, to my father, women demanded respect at all times, unless they acted in a disrespectful manner. Then, any means necessary was the measure—force being preferable. I shuddered at the thought. Visions flashed before me, hazed and muted. The sight shimmery. The scent scintillating. The scream sadistic.

I bent for a trunk, willing my mind to let go of the images and begin my adventure. The first thing I needed to do was find higher ground within the brush for my shelter, a safari style pop-up tent, complete with four-ply canvas protection from the predicted rains. I set to work, happy with the distraction.

++

A week into my banishment, I couldn't stand myself. I swam in the warmth of the crystal-clear Caribbean waters. I snorkeled like a pro discovering the beauty within the sea. I built a sandcastle like a child and slept on the beach under the blanket of stars, but I was bored out of my mind. Beginning to talk to myself, I worried I'd be making friends with a volleyball soon. If only I had one.

"As long as you don't decide to fuck it as well, you'll be good," I spoke to myself in second-person as if I might answer me.

I decided I needed to explore my surroundings better, learn the lay of the land like a voyager or the frontiers in the heritage of my family. Traditional compass in hand, I'd struggled through the week without electronic devices doing all the work for me. Nothing predicted the weather. No channels to surf for information on stocks or bonds or business in general. No GPS to point the direction for me. Holding the instrument securely in my palm, I trekked forward, marking my trail as I walked, making mental notes as I went in order to find my way back.

*This was all her fault*, I thought as I trekked. If she'd kept her mouth shut. If she hadn't gone after Rick. If the tape was never exposed, I wouldn't be on this island. My restoration coach, Garvey Edwin, was a graying-haired Native American who said I blamed everyone else for my predicament. *What did he know?* He wasn't there. He didn't feel the pressure to do as Rick said. He hadn't wanted to be a member of the club. The Front Door's secret society required what had been asked of me. I hadn't given it a thought, only acted. It was her fault she didn't play along.

I can't say I hiked more than a mile over rooted terrain and under lush foliage canopy when I came upon a natural spring and the rushing sound of a waterfall. The setting was picturesque—cascading white caps, crystal clear water, and a subtle ripple pressing outward. I wished I had a phone to capture the image, if only partially. Scanning the curtain of water as it fell from feet above to be captured in the filled rock basin, I discovered movement under the stream.

Suddenly a creature popped upward, startling me despite my concentration on the moving current. A dark head of slicked back hair rocketed upward as the upper body of the most peaceful, beautiful creature I'd ever seen appeared like a sea nymph released from the water. Rivulets of liquid caressed a solid, feminine back, licking sun-kissed skin. She spun and two delicious globes of perfection pointed at me. Each stood at attention, ripe to peaked-perfection and emphasized with the lushness of rosy nipples. Swiping back the sopping hair, delicate fingers caressed over a wet face of chiseled cheeks leaving behind an expression of calm serenity. Then lazy lids lifted and violet beams glared up at me. Startled, she screamed. And I recognized her instantly.

# 2

# Day 7 - Juliet

Paralyzed for a moment in my shock, several things transpired in the wake of sixty seconds. My eyes pierced the most gorgeous man I'd ever seen. A testament to glory and ancient gods, he stood on the edge of a rocky cliff, one knee bent upward as if staking his claim on a piece of land discovered solely by him. His hands hung at his sides in solid fists. The bulge to his long arms exuded strength. His hair was dark brown and mussed as if thick fingers recently combed through the strands, the tips kissed with sun-bleach. His eyes trained on my chest, dark and hollow in a face chipped as if by an expert in woodcraft, held me in place in my watery haven.

And then, I screamed.

The expression of his hard face transformed before me. His eyes opened wide. His mouth fell open. Startled. It was the only description of the look on his perfect face. And then it morphed, softening only briefly. His eyes flicked—the subtle motion a statement to something like recognition. Slowly his fists rose and unclenched, palms facing outward toward me. The sheer size of his mitts and the length of his fingers choked another scream from my throat. The second time, words followed.

"Go away."

With the sound of my voice, his head snapped backward, the slightest knock as if I struck him. Dark orbs within his sockets softened again. Then his cheeks hardened, the impression of wood returning. A tick at his cheek hinted at the clenching of back teeth. His eyes remained focused on my breasts, and my nipples tightened at the heat he exuded. I told myself it was the refreshing water still trickling off me, exposing my skin to the gentle air above the surface. I let him stare for just seconds before slapping my arms over my chest, tucking my hands under my pits. A shiver followed the movement, but it wasn't excitement that filled me.

It was fear.

And I refused to let it take me.

"Get the fuck out of here," I yelled as if he was a dog that could be chased away with words. He blinked and that wooden stare roamed my body. It felt lurid and luscious like a long lick, but I refused to acknowledge the tingle of pleasure. I denied it could exist in me.

"Get. The. Fuck. Away from me," I bellowed again, beginning to wonder if he was hard of hearing. Then wondering what he was doing on this island. The place was abandoned. I'd been told it would only be me. Small creatures, possibly. Millions of bugs, probably. But another human? Absolutely not.

"I'm not going to hurt you." A hoarse voice, tired and croaking from lack of use broke through the echo of my final demand. A tiny memory pricked at my brain, like a needle attempting to pop a balloon. Not quite through the surface of latex, my memory pressed back in resistance, refusing to allow penetration while it absorbed the sting. The hint drifted.

"I don't care," I barked. "Get out of here." My chest rose and fell, and I trembled uncontrollably. I could only imagine the sight of me—a woman on the edge of unhinging. My hair hung in clumps against my forehead. My throat stung with the weight of my scream. The tips of my fingers dug into the hollow pits under my arms. I felt my heart racing under my skin.

He continued to stare down at me, like a great mystery, a puzzle to be solved. I held my stance, glaring up at him despite the sun rays trickling through the leafy foliage behind him, haloing his head like he was some historical voyager, honored for staking out new land. He looked at me like unclaimed property, but he'd be wrong. I'd already been occupied. I'd been raped and pillaged, plundered and used. Unoccupied by permanence, like an abandoned homestead, I'd been depleted of anything considered a natural resource. He could not live off me. I'd kill him, choke him on the poison that surged through my body, feeding my hatred of all things male.

"Get—" The word seethed from behind my teeth, hissing in a reptilian sound of pure displeasure, yet his abrupt twist cut short the rest of the venomous sound. Without a word, he spun toward the trees, and stepped upward, exuding an effortless stretch of his long legs as he climbed the rocky outcrop, pulling himself to the next level. He didn't turn back—not even a slight glance over his shoulder to see if I watched his retreat.

If I recognized sadness, I'd think my heart pinched as he ignored me. His broad back rose over the rocks, dragging his muscular legs with him, carrying him away from me. But sadness no longer resided in me. I only wanted peace. I'd passed through the levels of despair. Forgiveness was the only step left to take. Learning another person lived on this island stood in my way. Realizing it was *him* made it worse.

# 3
## The Island Smells Your Fear

*How could she be here?* Of all things evil in the universe, her presence was the ultimate in betrayal. He'd been told—*no*, warned—there would not be another soul in existence on the island. Banished, alone, one year. That was the sentence. He'd accepted the terms in hopes to find inner harmony. His mind wrestled nightly with her face under his. His ears echoed with her silent pleas. His heart ached with what he'd done.

*She couldn't be here.* Not her, of all people.

Anger welled inside him to the point of detonation by the time he reached his waterside camp. He'd hacked at the low brush and pounded fists into small trees. He kicked at thick trunks and slapped his thighs as he hiked back to his temporary home. Once there, he swept sand over his fire pit and threw the coffee pot still set within the morning coals. Black liquid flew through the air, raining down in a gentle stream. *How prophetic*, he laughed. Laughter, deep and rich and bitter, like the campfire coffee. The sky mocked him with black raindrops, he thought, just like the dark liquid in his soul, just like the heavy tears he once shed for all he'd done to her.

And all she'd done to him.

He hated her while his heart once broke for her.

Stripping off his shirt, he raced for the waters' edge. He stumbled as he pulled up his foot, attempting to remove a hiking boot, tugging at it while he hopped forward. He fell to his knees, the impact hard and jolting. It was then that he noticed how hard he was, the length of him stiff and struggling beyond the zipper of his shorts. Like a child's tantrum, his legs kicked outward, flinging a boot away from him. His other knee bent and he used the same aggressive effort to remove the second boot before throwing it to his left. He peeled off his socks, leaving them lying haphazardly around him. A flattened palm pressed the length of him, rubbing up and down the hardened rod, both cursing at the excitement and relishing the throbbing heat.

Without a care for his nakedness, he loosened his shorts and stepped out of them as he ran for the ocean bay. He sprinted as far as his feet would take him before he dove deep into the refreshing water. The warmth did nothing to dissipate the heavy feel of his erection and his thick hand wrapped around himself, tugging tightly at the length. His wrist moved in rapid motion, both adrenaline and hatred pumping through his veins.

*Her.*

His eyes closed and he restored the memory. She was under him, whimpering. Violet eyes, filled with liquid and pleading. Her mouth had been gagged after Rick took his turn. He wanted to do baser things to her, but the initiates were too hungry for their turn.

Her hands had been tied, but he could no longer remember if it was over her head or behind her back. His original plan had been to enter her from behind. He didn't want to see her face. He didn't want to commit her to memory. He wanted his turn so he could be a member.

But then he saw her. Really saw her face, horrified, and bruising from where Rick slapped her. Without thought, his hand caressed her cheek, and she whimpered, flinching to get away from his touch, but she had nowhere to go. He remembered cooing at her, shushing her strangled cry.

*I'm not going to hurt you.*

The words rang in his head, drowning out the water rushing around him, lapping at his waist as he stood in the ocean. He rubbed harder, faster, jerking at his erection with the memory of those eyes under his. That flickering moment where she believed he wouldn't hurt her or hoped he wouldn't. That thin sliver of trust that he might have missed had he not been so intently drawn to her eyes.

He remembered his mouth coming down to her lips. Lips that trembled under his. She tried to twist her head, but his fingers gripped her chin.

*Just one.*

He asked her, although he was firmly in a position to take what he wanted. He'd always taken what he wanted, but for some reason, he waited. Hesitated. Hopeful. One time, he wished to receive something

17

not asked for, not stolen, not assumed. Entitled. The word roared through his head. He'd been entitled to have what he wanted and just once he wanted to be caught off guard. He wanted to be given permission, instead of expecting it.

He looked at the top of the mountain island, a shadow in a presently clouding sky. The weight of his sin pressed down on him, like the knowing-eye of that peak, like the heaviness of his dick in his palm. He drew in a deep breath, nearly shaking with the need for release. A tropical breeze lashed out at him, forcing the water to swirl around him. He inhaled the thick fragrance, committing it to memory, just like his transgression. He'd forever equate that scent with the image of her springing upward from the water.

With that thought, milky substance burst forth, mixing with the salty liquid surrounding him, washing him internally clean of desire and externally of his sweaty memory. He had to have imagined her, he reasoned. His head hung forward, relief at the release. His legs quivered under the water, toes digging into the sandy bottom to reinforce his balance.

If fear was an emotion he recognized, he'd worry. He'd never worried about being caught. There was no repercussion, until recent events. He didn't acknowledge fear, not in the face of this island. The only thing that frightened him was the displeasure of his father, and even that was no longer a concern. He'd never live up to Terror Corbin, and he wasn't sure he wanted to any longer. The sensation he felt standing in the waist-deep ocean was slightly different. Like one drop of blood within five miles of a hungry shark, he sensed something out there drawn to him. Something dangerous. His body hummed, his dick growing hard again. He looked up at the range, the tip disappearing into the clouds. The jagged cap penetrated the downy mist, blending them as one. Sensing a storm coming, he felt the ominous weight of eyes watching him, and he jerked off again.

# 4

# Day 7 - Juliet

*How could he be here?* I screamed in my head, as I hastily raced for my clothing. I didn't bother dressing. Clutching my shorts and T-shirt to my chest, I hustled through the thick brush, as if escaping Eden. I turned back occasionally, confident he hadn't followed me, but concerned enough to question my sanity. Did I imagine him? *Please let that be the case*, I prayed.

But my fear held strongly to the belief that he had not been a mirage. He was very much real and stood solidly in the flesh. And he was on this island. I clambered up the rope rungs of my tree house ladder, tripping once or twice in my naked haste. I reached the landing and roughly pulled the collapsible ladder upward. On more than one occasion, I was grateful for the solid structure that would be my home for a year.

One stipulation of my confinement was a stable edifice to live in, not a flimsy tent. The tree house was roughly one story off the ground and built like a small fortress. A porch circled the structure, centered by a bulky tree trunk. Built like the marital bed of Penelope and Odysseus, my housing surrounded the hefty trunk, allowing me a solid roof over my head and firm flooring under my feet. Not to mention, protection by its height in the trees.

With the ladder raised, I fell to the porch, wincing as I collapsed on my naked butt. My heart raced faster than the winds of a hurricane. My breaths came ragged and hurried.

*Why?* I cursed. *Why would you do this to me?*

My first thought was my uncle—a man who despised the fact he inherited me and not financial compensation with the death of my parents. My parents were not rich by any means, and Uncle Forrest was the black sheep, a distant cousin, considered my only living relative when I was thirteen. He would have enjoyed the seclusion of me on this island. He'd tried to lose me often enough in the forests surrounding his trailer in the middle of Nowheresville, Alabama. The fact I went to him as a young teenager was a shock to both of us. I hadn't known he existed until I set foot on his metal doorstep. Too sleek for a trailer park, his slicked-back, black hair, trim goatee, and jet-black eyes tortured me.

"The Lord has punished me," he cursed once the Department of Child Services left me. Years later, he swore that same statement as he looked at me with dangerous intentions in his alcohol-laden eyes. The lure of his seductive entreaties repulsed me, and I couldn't wait to get as far from him as I could. When the trouble occurred, I needed a family member to agree to the conditions of my trial. He was all I had.

This island was a social experiment. As an anthropology major, I wanted to study people. I'd been lonely as a child, in a trailer park, removed from my former home and formal society. The possibility of a solitary life didn't interest me, but the psychological ramifications would make for an interesting Master's thesis. Too bad I'd committed a crime to earn me this punishment.

"The Lord has punished you," he offered in a self-righteous slur. His pretend-belief in something almightier than a bottle of liquor choked me. He believed karma captured me, as I never gave into his lewd intentions. *The Lord*, as he professed, caused the sin I endured. If only I had given in to him, I'd better understand the ways of a man and could have prevented what happened to me. Or enjoyed it.

I shivered in disgust, wishing to return to the pond, and wash clean all thoughts related to my uncle. But thoughts of the pond brought an even greater evil to my mind.

*Him.*

He was part of the collection of men who ruined my life. They took what didn't belong to them. Thoughts of their crime caused me to tremble, my body visibly shaking. Naked or not, I curled into myself, the tips of my breasts brushing my bare knees, and I rolled to my side on the hardwood porch. I had no more tears for those men, not even him. Deep green eyes had stared down at me. I closed my own with the crash of memory.

*"I don't want to hurt you," he had whispered, his eyes glassy and bright from whatever drug they'd taken. He'd positioned himself in a manner that the thickness of his excitement fell between my thighs but hadn't penetrated me yet. A hand came to my cheek but I flinched at his touch. His eyes sought mine, telling me something, asking possibly, but I couldn't think. For one split second, I wanted to believe he wouldn't hurt me. I silently pleaded with him to let me go, but the damage had already been done. Whatever he did to me next would be no worse than the first man. I couldn't speak. I couldn't defend myself.*

And with those thoughts, I vomited at the recollection before allowing darkness to consume me. The world went black with my memory.

# 5

# Day 13 - Tack

The snap of a twig roused me from dozing. The storm outside howled and the rain beat on the heavy canvas over my head, but that crack of wood was more than the trees whipping in the wind. I sat up abruptly, wiping a hand through my unruly hair. The island didn't offer barber services, I mocked, and my hair was growing out of control in the heat. I turned my head to the side, angled toward the tent opening and waited a beat. Listening for another sound of movement unrelated to the storm, it felt as if the wind had actually stopped, standing still and holding its breath just like me.

*Crack.*

The instant the noise echoed through my tent, I leaped for the entrance. Standing upright, I stared at the empty darkness, the low embers of my campfire still smoldering but drowned of color by the rainfall. Drops instantly soaked my hair. On the other side of the fire ring, the outline of a female body did not surprise me. It was as if she emerged from the darkness, sleek with curves, slick with the moisture of rain. Instantly, I went hard at the thought of her body. She'd been damp when I touched her, her body responding despite her struggle. The luscious bend to her hourglass form vibrated under my palm on that night. The memory was instantaneous and just as sharply retreated.

Angry energy vibrated off her. A snap of lightning illuminated the sky and the glint of metal at her side caught my attention. A long, serrated knife rested at her thigh, grasped in her tight, tiny fist as if an extension of her arm. My eyes shot up to her face, pinched and focused on me. She hadn't spoken, and seconds beat, slowing down my heart rate to a crab's crawl over sand. Her chest heaved but other than that, she did not move.

A thousand questions filled my head as I stared at her narrowed eyes. Rain plastered her hair to her forehead. Her damp clothes clung to her, accentuating an outline I'd experienced too hastily. The thought made my dick leap, standing erect at attention, but I doubted she was here for another pass with me. She'd made her intentions clear after that night—she killed my best friend.

"Have you come to kill me?" I muttered, uncertain if she could hear me over the patter of rain hitting the tent canvas behind me. I should have been afraid, but I wasn't. My heart rate accelerated with the thrill of her anger. She remained fierce in her stance, despite her smaller frame, her intentions clearly etched in her wet face.

I stepped toward her. Lightning crackled, again brightening the sky, and she flinched. The hesitancy cost her, and I rounded the fire ring. Her head rose. Her shoulders straightened, but I noticed her shiver.

"Come inside," I offered, hoping to lure her into my tent. The rain was cold, and she was soaked. She stood like a caged animal, ready to leap, and I used my softest tone to tempt her. "You're all wet." The innuendo was clear. The thought rose the hairs on my skin, and I smiled slowly in hopes to calm her. This smirk had worked a million times to earn women in my bed. My body hummed with the desire to have her. I didn't even give a thought to the knife at her side until she raised it level with her head.

Her chest rose with calculated breaths, but I held out my hand, offering to take the weapon from her. She didn't accept my offering, and we stood in a match of wills while the rain continued pelting our faces with sharp stings, like repeated slaps for attention.

*Look at me*, she seemed to say with the negative energy rolling off her skin.

*I want you to see me*, I responded with bitterness in my mouth.

Neither words were spoken aloud, but that slapping rain forced our intentions to speak.

I turned my back to her. A mistake when presented with a woman who held a weapon, but I expected her to follow me. If my death was what she wanted, she'd have to work for it. Curiosity got the best of me, and I spun to face her. To my surprise, she stood immediately behind me. She hadn't made a sound as if she floated over the ground. Her breath mixed with mine in the cool mist rain. Half a step and her breasts would drag over my chest. The solid length in my shorts stood erect and ramrod ready, hanging on a thread of desire to pull her into the tent and enter the warmth of a feminine body. The ends of my fingers curled with the need to grab her and tug her close to me.

She still had not uttered a word.

I risked that half pace and drew up against her. My lids closed with the nearness of her. My body vibrated as it craved a female instead of the large palm of my fist. Her warm breath came out harsh against my neck, her exaggerated exhale only increasing the tremors of my body.

"Why are you here?" The deepness to her voice was nearly a growl, guttural and irritated. It snapped me out of my fantasy. Was it possible she didn't recognize me? Could she have forgotten what happened? The thought was ludicrous. Even I knew the answer—no woman would forget what we'd done. That was Rick's purpose.

*Make her never forget you're in charge and make her demand to be taken again.*

I wanted admission into the club. Submission was the trend, and my dominant nature fed off the thrill. I needed to learn more. She was my first victim. I ignored her questioning tone. I would never forget her face. I'd already seen all of her, but not in a way a man should see a woman. The proof was on the tape. The one mentally engraved in my brain.

As if she read my thoughts, I sensed the slow rise of metal to my left. She dragged the long dagger dangerously close to my arm, slowly lifting it as if she were skinning an animal and taking care not to damage the carcass. Level with my neck, she paused. Her violet eyes alit with hunger, desiring revenge.

"Kill me," I hissed. Our hearts beat in rapid tandem. "Will that make it better for you?" My sharp words exhaled outward, brushing over her too close face. "You'll have one more death to live with." The final comment answered an unasked question. She knew me. She knew damn well who I was, and I knew her.

Her body visibly quaked under the pelting rain. Her clothes were saturated, leaving nothing to the imagination. I could almost see her heart beating under her skin. My thick hand came to her wrist, and I forced the knife to my neck.

"Do it," I whispered, spitting at her, allowing my words to wash her cheeks as they mixed with the rain. Her eyes leaped from her concentration on my neck to my face. The movement cost her. I lowered her raised fist and twisted her wrist, forcing her to spin, pinning her arm to her back.

This was the position I'd desired her on that night. I didn't want to look at her. I couldn't face her. But I had seen her. The universe had returned her to me, or some sick twist of fate wanted me endlessly tortured. A hundred things passed through my head. Curses and comments, lascivious and lurid. I wanted to own her again, but something stopped me. The press of her back to my chest or the racing of my heart caused me to pause. This cost *me*.

As my forehead lowered to rest on the back of her head, her head shot back, connecting with my nose. I dropped her wrist as a searing pain ripped upward to my skull. My eyes watered, and I sucked in a sharp breath.

"You—" I stopped myself from the obscenity. The idea of her as a caged animal returned. She was acting on instinct, I reminded myself.

"I wasn't going to hurt you," I said quietly to the space between us, as she had already escaped around the fire ring. Her retreat only taunted me. She was a little mouse, and I was a lion ready to pounce. She continued to run.

"Don't make me chase you," I threatened louder, watching her disappear between the heavy foliage. Instantly, she was lost, swallowed up by the thick greenery and a dark night, and I choked on my words. I didn't mean them. This was no longer a game. I wouldn't follow her. She had nearly killed me. She *wanted* to kill me. The thought made me pause.

"I didn't do anything wrong," I screamed to the jungle. My voice bellowed over the trees, hoping to God she heard me. I hadn't. No, *you didn't do anything*, echoed through my head, cursing me in reply.

"I'm sorry I didn't do anything," I added, muttering to the saturated sand below my feet. I *was* sorry, sorrier than I'd ever been.

# 6

# Day 14 - Juliet

My heart raced with each step I took tracing my path back to my tree house. An expert at trails, I'd learned my way around the forest when my uncle dropped me in the woods, hoping I couldn't escape the prison of trees. Call it photographic memory, or just dumb luck, but I always found my way home. Maybe dumb luck *was* the correct terminology as his trailer was no home. I hadn't really had a place of my own from the moment I was dumped on his door until I moved in with Chellie in Baltimore and took classes at the community college. She was the reason I had the job at The Front Door.

My pulse kept pace with the brisk pounding of my feet on the dark jungle floor. Secluded on an island didn't leave me without some amenities. A visit from my counselor was due in less than a week. Lillian Varga was going to hear from me. I couldn't stay on this island if he was here. Everything about him said he wanted to hurt me, and despite the knife in my hand, I couldn't bring myself to harm him. I'd already done the unthinkable.

Rick Fontaine had been a monster. The moment I entered The Front Door, I knew I shouldn't have been there. His eyes roamed my body like my uncle's once did. Power was written in the edge of his jaw. His dark, beady eyes reminded me of a bird of prey. But I needed the job, and Chellie assured me Rick was harmless. The Front Door was a reputable establishment—a hot spot of the local club scene with two full floors of five-star food and unique beverages. It was the third floor that worried me.

I had graduated to serving the upper level, but my advancement was muddled with mixed intentions. If I worked there, I needed to pay the fee. Initiation was given by Rick...and his friends. I wasn't a willing participant. And *he* had been one of them. His name was Tack Corbin. I remember seeing him under the red lights. Stoned on something. Drunk on another thing. He always had a woman hanging off his arm. I never understood why he needed to take me. He'd never shown one bit of interest in me prior to that night, but then again, none of them had noticed me other than Rick.

I shivered at the memory as I climbed the ladder to the comfort of my home. The vision of him was hard to shake. That moment in his eyes where he peered down at me, reaching for my gagged lips, and then without pressure, he breathed words into my mouth.

*I don't want to hurt you.*

I wanted to believe him, but I couldn't believe one word uttered from the lips of those men. Rick had his turn first. Tack was next. Who knows how many would have followed, if Brandon hadn't walked in. My heart sunk to my stomach at the thought of Brandon. Sweet, gentle Brandon who tried to befriend me. His smile innocent, his attention refreshing. I'd been damaged goods after Rick had his way. Brandon would never look at me the same. He would have thought I'd been willing, as most women who entered the third floor apparently were.

Ignoring the weight in my belly, I crawled onto my bed. I had removed my soaked clothing and lay with my palm over my racing heart. I hadn't realized I still clutched the knife in my fist until I undressed. I'd ran and climbed without releasing it as if it were an extension of me. Maybe it was, as I had transformed into a killer after that night. Murder wasn't my intention, but I killed nonetheless. And Rick had deserved so much more. They both had, but something stopped me from hurting Tack. Memories of that night morphed the two men. *He'd hurt me, hadn't he?* It had always been a question. My imagination hopeful that he hadn't; my memory positive that he had.

*"We're going to play this my way,"* he'd said against my lips. *"Blink if you understand me."*

Afraid to close my eyes, they rapidly blinked before opening as wide as would allow. I shut down after that, no longer able to feel my skin or sense penetration. It was better this way. Better to pretend, focus on something other than him and the cloth gagging my mouth.

In the darkness of my room, the oppressive weight of him returned to me. I could feel him over me, between my thighs, breathing into my neck as he spoke to me. I couldn't remember what he said. I didn't want to enjoy the pleasure he professed to give. But as I lay in the dark heat, in my jungle surroundings, my hesitant fingers tickled over my tight nipples, eventually pinching them into twin peaks. My body arched at the sensation and a ripple snaked to my belly. Warmth spread between my legs, and I separated them, allowing any hint of a breeze to caress my skin prickling with a strange need.

I didn't want to be thinking of him, but somehow, he was all I could see. Those deep green eyes as rich as the palm trees. I imagined him between my thighs, and this time he would not control me. Tender fingertips traced a line down skin prickly and needy. Fingers slipped into my own underwear, tracing over sensitive folds before finding that special spot. Tender flicks, pleasurable circles, wet heat, and I detonated. My head rose from the bed as I called out his name, despite wanting to kill him.

"I hate you," I yelled to the heavy heat of my room, then fell back on the bed, unsatisfied with the performance and in desperate need of a repeat. I stroked again, the pleasure rising, and I rearranged my memory to suit my needs. His fingers fluttered. His tongue flicked. His dick filled me, and I came a second time with the fantasy of it meaning something.

+ +

I woke with a start. The sound of a motorboat in the distance, rising above the general chirps and squeaks of the tropics around me. My bra and underwear were plastered to my moist skin. The night had been warm, and my hair stuck to my neck and forehead. I rose for my clothing and dressed sluggishly. My midnight self-seduction left me exhausted and drowsy. Climbing down from the tree fort, I prepared myself to meet Lillian at the supply dock, a spot where she visited every two weeks to provide canned goods, bottled water, and fresh linens.

"Our intention isn't for you to starve or even feel like a prisoner. This island is meant to bring you in touch with yourself. Forget your sin, reconcile with what happened, and figure out how to make yourself whole again." It was a social experiment, not a self-sacrifice. The experience wasn't very social, however. I'd been alone often enough in life to know how to exist with loneliness and not be lonesome. There was a difference. I'd been writing daily in the journals provided, and so far, it had helped. Anger. Devastation. Repression. Thoughts and emotions bled onto the pages. But still, I felt nothing. I hated myself even more for giving in to self-soothing with images of him.

I stood at the end of the wooden platform and found myself staring off into the distance. There was no motor boat. No counselor. Loose threads of hair danced in the gentle morning wind, caressing my cheeks. Off on the horizon was another island. *How far was it?* I wondered. *Could I swim to it?* I couldn't live on this island knowing he was breathing my air and swimming in my water. Not only was it my hatred of him, but that sneaky sensation that I was strangely tempted by him. He'd already taken what he wanted from me, and yet I wasn't satisfied he'd taken enough. It was my turn for taking, and I wouldn't be asking. He certainly hadn't.

# 7

# Day 15 - Tack

"She's here on the island," I snapped before Garvey even left the boat. He hopped into the knee-deep water and bent over the sideboard to reach for supplies. It was my first formal check-in. Every fifteen days, I warranted a visit. At first, I thought it would be to double-check I hadn't killed myself. After my first few days on the island, I looked forward to the visit for the ability to speak to another human being. Today, I was pissed.

"How could you place her on this island with me?"

"Who?" Garvey asked, the bulkiness of his weight struggling with the box of canned goods and dry mixes. I cursed the food. I wanted a hot shower and a fresh shave. Without a mirror, I was struggling to remove the heavy growth of facial hair. I didn't need to turn into an island Yeti. I didn't need to *go native*. I was here for soul-searching, which hadn't appeared.

"That girl. The one that I..." I couldn't finish the statement. I hadn't done anything. That had been my plea. I never penetrated her and careful examination of the videotapes could prove that. Instead, the evidence made me guilty. I'd disguised my movement so well, it appeared as if I entered her when I hadn't. Either way, the conditions of our surroundings and the intention of our group was clear. She was there to be taken.

"There's no one else on this island," Garvey attempted to assure me, but his voice was only half convincing.

"She's here. Over there," I pointed in the general direction of both the pond and her escape the previous night. I hadn't been able to find her, despite my daily wanderings through the trees. It was as if she appeared out of nowhere and disappeared just as easily. Garvey looked in the same direction and back at me. I swiped a hand through my hair, tugging at the longer ends in frustration. I didn't feel neat. I wanted to be clean.

"I hope you brought soap. Maybe you could help me shave," I demanded, treating Garvey like a servant instead of the moderator he was meant to be. His suggestion was how I got in this mess. His great-grandfather and mine have some long-standing agreement. If either family ever got in trouble, the other was to help or something like that. Some first settlers bullshit. Instead of jail, I'd been offered restorative justice. Without enough research, I took the offering. My father had assured me it was better this way.

"Shave yourself," Colton offered. The younger image of Garvey, slim and trim in his cappuccino skin, stared back at me with mischief in his dark eyes. We were practically the same age, but his eyes spoke of wisdom older than me. He followed his elder to my tent, carrying another box of supplies.

"Are you journaling?" Garvey asked in his steady monotone. "It will help with the illusions."

"I'm not seeing things," I snapped.

"Ganja will help with that as well," Colton chuckled as he passed me.

"Colton," Garvey warned.

"Kidding," said the younger native, but the thought piqued my interest.

"There's marijuana on this island?" I asked, looking off at the distant greenery that dressed nearly ninety-nine percent of the island.

"You tell me. You're the one who saw Mary Jane," Colton teased, raising his forefinger and thumb to his lips, signifying smoking.

"Fuck off," I barked, feeling surlier than normal this morning. Maybe it was the near-death experience that only caught up with me once she ran off. She'd fully intended to kill me last night. "I can't stay here." The words sounded weak. *Can't* implied incompetence. I wasn't a wimp, but I didn't wish to die either.

"Why not?" Garvey asked, peering up at me from the seat he'd given himself on the stump of a tree.

"She's here," I hissed again, sounding like a madman as the words escaped.

"Tell me about her," Garvey asked as he picked up a stick, took out a knife and began to scrape at the tender outer covering.

"She tried to kill me," I sighed. Colton's head shot up and he twisted to face his father.

"Why would she do that?" Garvey questioned, continuing to whittle, and I wanted to shove that stick up his ass.

"Because she's crazy." She'd already killed Rick. She wished death for me next.

"Is she?" Garvey muttered, and my anger grew.

"Fuck, yes. She came at me with a knife last night."

Garvey fumbled for a moment, and the stick snapped in half. A jagged edge pointed toward me.

"Would she have reason to kill you, if that were a solution?"

I pondered the question. Unequivocally, my first thought was no, but then the words haunting me since last night returned to me.

*I didn't do anything.*

I hadn't prevented anything from happening to her. I watched as Rick took his turn—sickened and anxious, awaiting my chance. Then I faltered as I pressed over her. Her eyes caught me so off guard. I played along, as I often did when Rick led. I followed his lead, forging my own rules behind him.

*We're going to play this my way.* I'd said the words to her, but I don't think she heard me. Her eyes glassed over after that. It was as if I watched her shut down under me. What would be the point of taking her, if she didn't remember me? Forcing myself into her pliable body wasn't going to etch me in her memory. This wasn't how I expected the club to be. I knew it was only Rick's initiation or some kind of sick game. And once again, I'd given in. I don't know why I found a conscience in those few minutes.

"I don't think so," I lied, feeling the weakness of my words on my lips. I spit in reaction as if I could remove the disgusting taste from my mouth.

"Huh," Colton said, and I looked up to find his taunting eyes sparkling. He was about my size, and I wondered if he'd consider a tussle. I could use the beating, or better yet, to beat on something.

"Don't *huh* me," I barked again, fists forming at my sides. Colton's smile only grew, curling larger, brightening his clean-shaven face. I hated how put-together he looked. I stepped forward, and Colton unfolded from the sand where he had sat down next to his father.

"Stop it," Garvey snapped, pointing his mini-jackknife in my direction. "This isn't helping you. You need to get over your anger. Learn to control it, not invite it in. That's how you got into this mess in the first place."

"It wasn't anger that got me here," I retorted. Sex was the reason, but I didn't offer that explanation. As if reading my thoughts, Garvey responded.

"Anger was the very thing and nothing else. Taking a woman against her will is about control. Angry control. Anger repressed and out of control. Possibly anger toward someone who controlled you." Each statement ticked down a figurative list, and my body tensed with each comment.

"I'm not angry," I growled, giving proof that I was. I swiped a hand through my unruly hair once again. "Just get me off this island. Get me into anger management counseling or something." I tried to smile, willing the muscles to raise my lips in my false plea. I wasn't going to any damn shrink. My mother had been in and out of therapy for years and it had done nothing for her, but aide her addiction to pretty-colored pills.

"That wasn't an option. Jail or the island. You picked here."

I didn't choose. I wasn't given a choice. My father thought it best for the company if I came here, like a vacation or a sabbatical, not a punishment. I was promised I couldn't be traced. No one would know other than Garvey, Colton and the restorative justice team. But *she* knew I was here, and this brought me full circle.

"I can't stay here with her."

"Then get her out of your head. Start journaling." With that Garvey rose, and Colton followed. They didn't believe me. She wasn't a hallucination; she was an in-the-flesh human being. The thought struck me as sharp as the wood Garvey whittled and stuck in the sand—she was an innocent person, and I'd tried to take from her as I always had.

+ +

*I hate you*, I wrote in the journal. That was the most I had to say on paper in the three days after Garvey's visit. I blamed her for my being on this island. I cursed her for disappearing again. I'd searched for her, wandering the trails I'd formed from my tent oasis to the pond and around it. There was no sign of her existence, and I questioned my own sanity. Had I imagined her after all, as Garvey suggested? Was I hallucinating without any substances?

I lay in my tent for the third stifling night, wanting to keep the tent flap open for air and knowing I couldn't because of things that go bump in the night. I hadn't been frightened of the island once, until the reality of her standing there, knife raised, brought into perspective that she wanted me dead. There were moments in my life I'd wished the same thing. The time my father raised his hand to me. The time I found my mother on the bathroom floor with pills beside her. The time I sat handcuffed in a holding cell.

This was all *her* fault.

The thought brought me up short. Was it really her fault? Had she put me in that cell? Had she forced me to lay on top of her? Had she handed me the drink I took from Rick that night? My questions didn't need an answer and didn't receive one, as the sharp rip of the tent zipper jerked me to the present. The flap was forced back, and she stood before me. I had only a moment to make out her silhouette. In her hand, she held a flashlight, and I pondered the amenity. Intrigue over a flashlight didn't last long as she straddled my outstretched legs and slapped me hard with the flat of her hand. The sharp crack stung, and my cheek vibrated.

"What the fuck?" I hissed, prepared to grip her wrists, proactive against another attack, when the flashlight went dark, tumbling to the ground and submerging us both in deep black. A second hand came to my face. Not gentle, but not a slap. Rough fingers cupped my jaw and a thumb traveled my cheek before latching onto my lips. In an instant, her mouth was on mine, hard and fast—not a kiss but an assault, that was clumsy and hesitant, yet determined. Her core rested over a slowly growing length, rutting back and forth over my zipper. She pulled back to nip at my lips. She moved downward to bite my jaw. She pulled back as shaky fingers skittered down my bare chest and fumbled for the waist of my shorts.

"What the hell?" I snapped, unable to see her, but feeling her thighs on either side of mine. My hands reached out and found bare legs. Pressing upward over warm skin, the edge of a long shirt tickled the backs of my hands. Her hips rocked aggressively over me, and my body betrayed all sense. This girl was going to kill me any second, and I was going to die with a hard-on.

Her fingers dug into the waist of my shorts, tugging back on the heavy cargo material before the subtle popping sound gave testament to a button released. She scooted back only enough to pull at the sides of my shorts, and I sprang forth into air heavy with heat and the scent of arousal surrounding me.

"What are you doing, Little Mouse?" My voice rumbled, low and rushed.

"I am not a mouse," she snapped, gripping my dick with a hot palm and tugging aggressively. The pleasure was painful. My little mouse was rough. One hand wrapped over hers, the other clasped her hip and flipped her so I was over her. My hips rocked forward, guiding her hand with mine to slow the pace as she stroked me into a thick, stiff rod.

"No," she hissed, rough fingers squeezing my hard length. She freed her other hand and pressed back on my chest, intimating she wanted control. I didn't release her hand that was rapidly jerking over me, but I dug my knee into the mattress and flipped us back over so she could straddle me once more.

"What do you want, Little Mouse?" I chuckled humorlessly. Thoughts of her suddenly stabbing me did not deter me from forcing her to tug my dick. Her tiny fingers encapsulated in mine, working over sensitive skin and a hard shaft was my only focus. Without words, she rocked back and stood my erection upward. The heat of her core balanced on my tip before she forced her body downward, enveloping me inside her wet warmth.

"Ah," we grunted in unison. Whether the response was the sharp pain of my entrance or the pleasure of filling her to the hilt made no difference to the sensation curling over my toes and down my spine. It'd been months since I entered a woman, and my eyes rolled back at the euphoria. She drew to the tip once again and impaled herself on my hard length, grunting and rutting out of control, animalistic in spite of her tiny frame. A little mouse gyrating over me, nibbling at my essence as she swallowed me intimately inside her, clenching, clutching, squeezing.

"Jesus, fuck." My fingers dug into her hips, holding her against me as she rode up and down. Her nails crawled down my chest, raking divots into the freshly sun-kissed skin. In the darkness, my eyes adjusted, and I was able to make out the shape of her head, tipped back in ecstasy.

"Do you like this, Mouse?" One hand came for my face again, but I caught her wrist. Tugging her outstretched palm to my lips, I kissed the inside of her flattened hand. "I like this," I hissed as she worked frantically over my length, ripping from me an orgasm that raced from my lower back and burst forth into her. I clutched her hips, forcing her to hold still as I pulsed into her. Her hips struggled to rock, and I realized she was close but not there yet. She wanted control but I wanted her pleasure.

I slipped my palm over her flat belly and stretched my thumb to find that sensitive nub I thought might set her off. Circling the pad over the tender folds, she screamed. Her fingers dug into my sides, pinching my skin as her head rolled forward. Her hair draped down and tickled my chest. The only sound was the echo of our breaths, ragged and rapid in the heat of a tent filled with the rich aroma of sex.

Slowly, her hands released me to lay flat on my stomach. She pushed back her hair and I felt the weight of her eyes on me, despite the darkness. I could only feel her features, not see them. I wanted to read her face but it was shielded from my vision. Our chests still rose and fell in unison, the excursion settling slowly. My eyes closed with exhaustion, but a smile crossed my face. Languid and drained, I sighed as I slipped out of her, semi-hard, but needing a moment before I could take her again. My hands slid down her bare thighs and brushed her knees on either side of my hips.

"Mouse," I whispered before I fell into the deepest sleep I've had in months.

# 8

# Day 20 - Juliet

The sound of water falling flowed behind me as I soaked in the pond. Nature's lullaby surrounded me with the chorus of birds and the rustle of a breeze. Lillian had warned me the fresh water would be cold, but emptying my mind would change the temperature.

"Become one with nature. Free yourself," she told me after she first brought me to the island. "The power to change lies within you."

On her most recent visit, she mentioned that I'd lost weight. She looked concerned, but I assured her I was fine. I wasn't giving up on the experiment. I wasn't ready to return home. I had more to learn about the island and myself. I don't know why, but I didn't mention my island neighbor.

*Have you experienced anything unusual on the island?*

I should have told her, so when she appeared one visit and I was dead, she'd know who'd done it. Cupping water in my hands, I poured it over my head, hoping to rid my thoughts of him. He had stared at me with venom in those eyes. I'd had the strength to kill once before, but I lost my willpower the night I hoped to take him. *Kill me.* His tone reeked with a hint of desire for the deed to be done. Something in his stance expressed his hope to be finished. *But finished from what?*

I suspected a boat came for him, and I was surprised he hadn't left. Maybe he was in the same social experiment as me, but I doubted he'd volunteered. I knew of him only from the club. Some billionaire playboy—Daddy's protégé—entitlement and money. Things I didn't care one lick about in the grand scheme of life, but I couldn't keep my eyes from him then. I only wanted a fresh start for myself and had every intention of fulfilling that goal until that night.

I closed my eyes as I settled into the cool liquid. I would not think of such things as that night, Rick Fontaine, or Tack Corbin. While his eyes haunted me behind my lids, I emptied my mind of all other things related to him. I would not think of his firm thighs. I refused to give into the pressure of his hands that lingered on my hips. I rejected the hungry taste of his lips.

My body eased into the watery haven as I inhaled deeply and released slowly. Letting my arms drift caused subtle ripples and I willed the tension of my body to dissipate. My arms floated before falling to dead weights and coming to rest next to my sides. I sat on a natural ledge within the pond and my legs flexed before unknotting the tension in them. I became one with my surroundings and aware of my breathing.

Not certain how long I stayed in this state, my mind flipped through memories like a picture book. Each negative thought turned over like an unread page. A snapshot of my parent's two caskets. An image of the sinister smile on my uncle's face. A photograph of Rick's body draining of blood. A video of me withering from the intrusion of his body. I did not wish to review my life. I just wanted to sit. I longed for peace.

I might have dozed. And then I felt a presence—the weight of being watched. My lids lazily opened, revealing my predator on the rocky cliff above me. He stood as he had the first time I saw him, but this time I did not scream. The coldness of the water rushed over me as the connection with nature was broken, but I did not flinch in the chilly pond.

*The power rests in me*, I told myself.

He didn't speak, only stared, our eyes connecting over the valley of space. The rush of water from the fall behind me softened, slowly slipping away. The brightness of the day heightened, illuminating him. My body felt so tranquil, even his domineering stance would not rouse me from my calm. I stood slowly, letting the water cascade down my shoulders and over my breasts, dripping off the sharp, cold peaks. As I stood, he lowered to a crouch. He appeared perched to pounce, but I reminded myself I was in control. His eyes remained on me. I told myself he was bowing to a queen.

My hands rose to swipe back my damp hair, the movement accentuating my breasts, forcing them forward. More water rippled off of them and his eyes didn't leave the display. I slipped my fingers across my chest, reaching for each opposite shoulder in preparation to cover myself and then decided against it. He would not control me. A sense of empowerment flooded through me, and I lowered my palms, allowing each to caress a breast. Cupping myself, the weight of heavy globes filled with achy need, peaked by the heated desire in his eyes. The subtle roll of his throat alerted me to his struggle. He hungered for me.

After pinching each nipple, my hands skated down my sides, dipping below the water line that covered the tip of curly, black hairs. I left him no doubt where those fingers traveled, and I focused on him as I stroked over tenderly bruised skin. I'd worked my own flesh too often lately, but I couldn't give up the strength I felt watching him, watching me.

The pressure built slowly as each finger took a turn combing over deep folds. The cold water was a new sensation as I concentrated on it, like a refreshing breeze between my thighs or a soft rush of breath from a lover. I'd never experienced love before, but I imagined gentle touches would be part of it. I didn't want to look away from him, but the intensity of the green eyes narrowed on me forced my eyes to close. The spell wasn't broken. Circular brushes and the ripple of water between my thighs increased the slow build-up. The crawl of pleasure took its time, fluttering down my belly and licking up my legs before releasing from me. One hand reached forward for the rocky backing to this natural ledge. Steadying myself, my fingers continued to separate me as I took sharp, short breaths with each clench. Finally subsiding, a sense of peace came over me. My legs quaked. Slowly, I lifted my head.

He sat in a relaxed position, perched on one hand, looking down at me. His expression stoic, his eyes danced, sparkling in the reflection of the sunshine. I bit the corner of my lip, refusing to give him the smile fighting to curve my mouth and hint at my satisfaction. Empowerment reigned over me. My fingers retreated from between my thighs, and I turned for the water's edge opposite him. Climbing out of the pond, I did nothing to hide my naked body. I bent at the waist, giving him a full view of my backside as I picked up my clothing. Then, I walked away from him.

# 9

# Day 20 - Tack

Mother of all things holy and more, that was the sexiest thing I'd ever witnessed. If I considered her a water nymph on our first meeting, this performance proved she was the goddess of temptation. If I thought I dreamed her coming into my tent and taking what she wanted from me, the look of her in broad daylight proved she was more than a fantasy. Rock hard and gripping the real rocks under my palms, I watched her display, taking pleasure in the show without touching myself for the release I craved. I worried the slightest movement might interrupt her, and I wanted to allow her this moment. She stood like a mythical creature, ensnaring me in her game of show not tell. The rapture on her face made me ache and I was thirsty for a taste. I wanted to drink in her expression and witness it again and again. But then she walked away.

I should have followed her, but I didn't trust my legs. My body vibrated with the need to expel the pent-up orgasm, but I relished the tremble. She had me, and I didn't suppress the smile as she stalked away. I'd never wanted anyone as much as I wanted her. Physical. Raw. Aggressive. Her body would fulfill mine in a hundred ways and more, but I didn't want to take her that way. The steady strength exposed as she took her time to please herself, the way she slowed her pace, filled me with a strange desire to fill her repeatedly in a manner that would reproduce the peaceful rapture I witnessed moments ago. Her lips parting. Her eyes closing. Her body causing slow ripples in the water. Sensual and innocent, I wanted a piece of it.

My eyes followed her path, but I knew I'd lose her again. I assumed she wasn't much farther than the pond, and I wanted to make this a regular stop in my daily discovery of the island. If she was all I saw each day, I would consider myself a fortunate man. As my heart rate lowered, and my erection subsided, I found the strength to stand. This day was the day to track her, and I crossed the upper edge of the rocky cliff to trace her retreat.

++

Unfortunately, I found nothing. For three days, I came to the pond and found it empty. And for three days, I took all manner of directions on the opposite side in search of her. I wandered through foliage so thick it suffocated me, triggering a claustrophobia I hadn't had prior. One day I reached an open space of sparsely situated trees. I stood a moment, feeling lost both literally and figuratively, even though I sensed I'd been in this spot before. I'd tried to journal again and had only gotten as far as writing—*she is a wonder to me*. Three days without her orgasmic display, and I'd come to terms with wanting to learn more about her as a person, not just physically.

I paced in a small circle, placing my hands on top of my head. My eyes focused on the soft, black dirt under my feet. That's when I saw it. A subtle imprint of a fire circle, the ashes scattered to cover the evidence. My neck twisted, spinning me right and left as I searched through the trees.

"Come on," I groaned, looking up to the barely visible blue sky. Two fists gripped my shaggy, unkempt hair and then I saw it. A platform part way up a tree. I stepped back to take a better look. There, in the middle of the tree line, a platform of sorts circled a trunk, highlighting it as the center. A square in one spot suggested a ladder might descend to the ground to allow occupants. Otherwise, there was no other visible way to get to that height than the proximity of other trees and some thick vines hanging between them. How very *Tarzan*ish, I thought as a smirk graced my face. I'd walked this place a few times before and never noticed that she'd been above me all this time.

# 10

# Day 23 - Juliet

A strip of vibrant blue, star-shaped flowers lay at the threshold of my door. For a moment, I thought they'd fallen there or possibly been blown onto the landing, but the flowers lay too perfectly posed. Bending, I picked up the ribbon of blue blooms and rubbed the stem between my fingers. I couldn't recall the image of this particular flower from the list of poisonous ones Lillian had given me. The beautiful cascade of five petals spun in my fingers—simple, brilliant, unique—and I inhaled a sweet fragrance, having no other word to describe it than tropical.

The thought gave me pause, and I looked over the low railing of my abode. Searching the ground below, I suddenly questioned how he'd found me and how he'd climbed my tree. The ladder was pulled each time I entered for security. More so for safety, since I knew of his presence. I thought back to the other day, his eyes on me as I touched myself. He was a predator, and I was still his prey. Was he enjoying the chase, or did he no longer hunt me? His gaze seemed intrigued as well as appraising, but that could have been my imagination. Just like I imagined he wanted to protect me that terrible night in the club.

I re-entered my tree house and dropped back on the bed. I'd drawn up the mosquito netting, allowing the air to circulate easily over me. I'd been writing for days, collecting my thoughts on the surroundings of the island and the concept of living a solitary life. Without a computer, the writing was painstakingly slow. Handwritten journals were tiring, yet strangely refreshing. Growing up electronics-free, I didn't have a cell phone until high school. I never owned a computer until after I applied for my Master's degree. I wanted to be a scientist of people—an anthropologist. How quickly life changed.

In my journal, I wrote about my fear of others, although I hadn't been attacked by a gang, just a small group of surly, drugged men who wanted a plaything for one night. My fear was something that Lillian promoted in order to secure my placement—she refused to call the island a punishment.

*"We recommend Juliet for this experiment. She's the perfect candidate. She has no prior felonies or convictions. Jail time would be a detriment to her. If this process is to reflect and renew, we believe she has the intellect and compassion to follow through."* The 'we' Lillian mentioned was herself, as my mentor, my uncle was the sole family member, and my probation officer. Jared Michaels had been the one to bring the restorative justice experiment to Lillian's attention.

*"It's a program of rehabilitation. It's not a punishment, but a reformation. Not punitive but restitution. A person must buy into the process, like AA or drug rehab, and Juliet has the commitment. This is her consequence. She made a poor decision. How will she make whole on that choice?"* Jared was a Native American descendant of the Algonquin First Nation, and proud supporter of the Native heritage in modern times. As a public defender, he'd been known to bring Native practices into courtrooms as a way to give retribution to both victim and offender.

I was the offender.

After I'd been a victim.

*"You made a choice, Juliet. A poor one, albeit understandable. Restorative justice will question the anger that drove you to make the decision you made,"* Jared stated.

The decision, as Jared casually called it, was the result of additional harassment. I'd promised not to tell anyone what happened. I didn't have anyone to tell anyway. Who would believe me? I worked at a club notorious for dealings in dominance and submission, although only a select group knew of such happenings on the third floor. Chellie reminded me I wanted to work that level. When I discovered the third floor, I should have turned the other way. I should have never offered to serve up there, but I wanted the financial raise. And my curiosity was piqued. This was another culture of people, and the scientist in me wanted to know more without coming off like a creep.

It was over my head, as I too quickly learned. Despite my assurances that I'd never speak of what happened, Rick sought me. He wanted me to come back to the club after I quit.

*"Did you like it?"*

*I thought ignoring his question would prompt him to walk away from me as I stood near the bar, waiting to collect my final paycheck.*

*"Would you like to do it again?"*

*The tease to his voice raked on my nerves. Blood boiled inside me as my body pulsed with fear. I grabbed the closest thing—a paring knife used to slice up lemons and limes. Stepping closer to the enemy, as I'd read on a self-defense website, I looked up at him, holding my emotions at bay as best I could, surprised that I fooled him. For a brief second, he looked as if he believed I might agree to another round. As if I'd ever want a second chance at how he treated me. As if I'd let other men do the same thing to me, in that position, in that manner. My clenched fist rose, and drawing on strength I didn't know I had, I stabbed him in the neck, cutting through his jugular.*

Yes, I'd made a choice—swift and rash—but so had Rick Fontaine.

There's a moment in napping where you sense where you are, you're aware of your surroundings, but you're so deeply in a dream or memory, you can't move. I was in that state, feeling the pressure of Rick's hands on my ankles, forcing my legs apart, the weight of his palms over my calves like the clammy underbelly of a snake. The rhythmic inching of his fingers coming closer to a part I did not wish him to enter.

A hissing sound mixed with Rick's voice.

*"Do you…siss…like this…siss?"*

My eyes flicked open, and I screamed in response.

# 11

# Day 24 – Tack

I heard the blood-curdling scream despite the distance. This wasn't a woman frightened by a mouse, but someone in imminent danger. *Juliet.* I dropped my journal and raced in the direction of her tree house. Listening as I hurdled over small brush and crushed twigs under my feet, I waited for another sound that didn't happen. I held my breath as I ran the longest two miles in my life. My pace quickened each second there wasn't another bellow, and fear grew that whatever I'd find, I'd be too late. I had no assurance the cry came from her tree house, but I didn't know where else to start. Nor did I have a sense of the direction her cry occurred. I shouted her name with no response. With us as the only two human residents on this island, sound was distorted under the treetops.

"Fuck," I cursed, as I neared her home, finding the ladder removed. "Juliet?" I yelled, hoping she would give me some sound, some recognition that she heard me. A crash above my head had me rushing toward the tree I'd climbed to reach her balcony. I launched myself from the closest tree to the vine I used to propel myself over her railing. Dropping onto her balcony, I wasn't prepared for what I saw.

A large, speckled snake dangled above her.

Not being versed in the great outdoors, I had no idea the type, other than the length seemed endless and part of it lay in a ribbon across her legs. The head was above her, its body coiled over the natural rafter of a large tree limb.

"Juliet," I whispered, uncertain how I was going to save her. She didn't whimper or sigh or blink. For a moment, I wasn't certain she was still alive, but then the lizard-like tongue slithered from its mouth, and Juliet squeaked.

The knife she'd used on me lay on a stand next to her bed and my only thought was to somehow sever the head of this creature, hoping it wouldn't strike her before I could make it through his thick skin.

So mesmerized was the creature by Juliet, it didn't sense my movement as I neared the bed. With her legs trapped and her fear paralyzing her, I didn't know how I was going to get her to move, but I aimed for what I assumed was the neck directly behind the eyes and struck.

Blood rained down on Juliet, but the head remained mostly intact. It lowered and fear surged through me that it would lash out at her. Several things happened in tandem.

"Roll toward me," I demanded, as I braced to step on the frame of the bed and launched the knife at the wound of its head. She could only twist the upper portion of her body but it was enough. The snake shot forward at the movement, and I stabbed again, forcing the head away from her.

The body was retreating as the head dangled obscenely from the base. His tongue slithered forward, eyes matching the devil. He was dissected, but not dead. I hacked one more time and the head fell to the bed, narrowly missing Juliet's hip. I stood over her like a savage hunter, legs spread and straddling her body. Quickly, I kicked the head away from her and bent to push the surprisingly heavy weight of the body off her legs. Her knees bent, and she kicked out at the remaining loops of its body as well. Then she leaped from the bed and ran for her door.

"Juliet," I cried, quickly following after her. One hand reached for her upper arm, catching her before she crossed through the exit. "Juliet, did he get you? Are you okay?" I spun her to face me, and without thought, drew her to my chest. The warm blood on her cheeks drenched my shirt, the stench overwhelmingly rancid. She pushed on my chest with a force that surprised me into releasing her and scrambled in the opposite direction. She collapsed and huddled on the floor near a small chair.

"Juliet," I whispered as I slowly approached her. Her knees drawn upward with hands over her head, I witnessed her fear, a tangible presence hovering over us. She was trying to cover herself as if she could disappear in this position. Her body trembled, forcing her slender knees to knock against one another.

"Juliet," I whispered again as I lowered to a squat, softening my voice as if I spoke to a child. I had no practice with children, but I tried to keep my tone tender. My hand reached forward despite my hesitation. I circled her wrist in hopes to remove her hands from her head. She flinched but I tightened my hold. The effect was what I wanted. She looked up at me, eyes wild and glassy, her face spattered with blood.

"It's okay. You're okay. I'm not going to hurt you."

Her head shook and tears leaked from her eyes. She seemed too strong to cry. She hadn't cried *that* night. She hadn't cried when she came to kill me. Witnessing the delicate streams trickling down her thin cheeks crushed me in a way I'd never felt before.

"I'm sorry," I whispered, my voice so low it cracked, and I knew she hadn't heard me. She hadn't been afraid that night, or at least she didn't show it. But she was frightened now, and I couldn't decide if it was the snake or me she feared. When she looked away from me, I dreaded the thought was the latter.

Shifting to my knees, I reached forward and wrapped my hands around her shoulders, the quake of her body so evident she vibrated under my touch as I lifted her. I shifted a second time and instantly dragged her into my lap, enveloping her by circling her back and rounding my other arm over her tight knees that were pressed to her chest. She was so frail, yet I did not consider her weak. She fit over my thighs, and I drew her to me. Her head fell to my shoulder. I didn't think before I kissed the top of her head where her hair met tanned skin. Keeping my lips there, I whispered again.

"I'm not going to hurt you. Nothing will ever hurt you again."

+ +

I'd returned to my tent after lifting the dead snake head and launching it into the jungle. We worked in tandem, and in silence, as we removed the dead weight of the snake body, disengaging it from its position coiled around the limb rafter. I wanted to comment on her lodging, but each time I opened my mouth for a sarcastic comment, I would see the hollow look in her eyes and the blood still splattered on her face.

Her shelter was stable, with a small bed made of tree trunks and other furniture framed by bamboo. She'd argued with hand motions that she would take care of the linens, refusing my attempt to strip the bed, but I refused to ignore the mess. There was nothing processed or pressed in her place, only the natural wood of our surrounding. *Was she resourceful? Had she made these things? How did she get them up here?* These ridiculous questions occupied my mind as I worked beside her.

She'd made no other sound than a grunt or a grimace. Darkness began to creep into the trees, and I didn't want to leave her but I didn't know how to stay. I feared the stench of death would draw other creatures to her shelter, but she refused my suggestion.

"You could come to my tent," I offered, standing near the door as I watched her stare out the window into the growing night. She shook her head. Her arms crossed over her chest, hands clutching her elbows. She looked broken, and I wondered briefly if she'd looked like that after what we did, after what she did. She was no longer innocent of crime, but this near-death experience brought a strange sense of perspective.

"I'll…" I didn't know what to say, letting my voice falter. *I'll see you around* seemed a little blasé for what we'd both just been through.

"Thank you," she whispered without removing her eyes from the open window. I continued to stare at her after she spoke.

*Ask me to stay*, I thought, wondering where the question came from. It wasn't that her place was better than mine, but that I didn't want to walk away and leave her unprotected. Saving her life had made me feel strangely obsessed with protecting her.

Without further acknowledging me, I left.

By the time I entered my tent, I was irritated. My journal lay open, pages bent on the floor of my flimsy housing and I swiped it up in my agitation.

*You ruined my life*, I'd written. The statement made me pause. *Had she?* I wanted to lay blame on Rick, on her. If she hadn't killed him, the tape would have never been revealed. The video was evidence of what he'd done to her, and I became an accomplice. If she'd kept her mouth shut like she promised, neither of us would be on this island and Rick would be alive. I don't know why she had to kill him. Threaten him, yes—many women had done that before. Scream at him, definitely. Slap him, like she smacked me. He might have laughed in her face. *But kill him?* I shook my head. That had been extreme.

I stared at the words I'd written.

Knowing she nearly died from that snake made me think. That reptile acted on instinct. While it was ready to make Juliet his dinner, she was his source of survival. Her fear fueled his desire to have her. Her innocence made her an easy hunt. Rick Fontaine had been a hunter—he preyed on the weak. Hadn't he done the same thing? He thrived on the capture, but why Juliet? The answer was simple: she refused him, and it drove his desire to conquer. Had Juliet reacted to him in her own sense of survival? Had she killed him before being killed, as is the nature of animals? Was she that base? *Was I?*

I sat with a thump on my mattress which was covered by a sleeping bag and a sheet. Sleeping on a pallet only inches from the ground was nothing like the luxury of her bed. This was part of my punishment—stepping back to basics and living without things. But Garvey had told me it was deeper than giving up items.

*"Circle justice was a way of practice for my people. If you commit a crime, you must make things whole again. If you killed a dog, you might need to adopt a puppy or work at an animal shelter."*

*"I didn't kill a damn dog,"* I argued, and he scowled at me like I was an imbecile.

*"You must decide why you harmed and then what you plan to do about it to make things better."*

I scoffed at the idea. *I didn't do anything*, I argued. *I didn't need to make anything better. This was her fault. She needed to make things better for me.*

Everything had been done by Rick, but the judge didn't see it that way, and I'd taken the deal only to avoid jail time. I didn't want to become someone's bitch. But what Garvey said made a bit of sense.

He'd muttered something about *what you do to the animals you do to yourself.* I didn't understand his meaning, but witnessing the snake attacking Juliet changed things. Why did it want to harm her? Strangely, I understood Rick. He had a desire to possess, but I didn't know where the root of that obsession came from. I didn't know where it came from in me, and because of that, I had no answer as to how I'd make things whole. Did I owe Rick or Juliet? Rick was dead. I couldn't bring him back. My chest ached at the thought that if the snake killed Juliet, I would not be able to repair her, either.

# 12

# Day 28 - Tack

I opened the flap to my tent to find Juliet sitting on the shore facing out toward the sea. For days, I'd been to her tree house, pacing under the landing like a lovesick Romeo, silently sending out pleas for her to drop the ladder and let me up. Maybe that chick with the long hair was a better analogy. Juliet seemed to lock herself in a tower and was refusing to see me.

Sitting on the white sand outside my tent seemed strangely unnatural as if she didn't belong here with me. I shook my head. The thought made no sense. I walked to where she sat and plopped down next to her. My feet stretched forward and my hands fell back, giving me the casual appearance of a man at the beach. I stared out at the water, waiting for her to speak.

And I was ready to come out of my skin because it had been four days since I'd seen her. Her silence unnerved me. Taking a side glance, I noticed she looked tired. Deep purple bags hung under her eyes. Her knees were brought upward, but her arms casually wrapped around her shins.

"You have a better view than me." It wasn't what I expected her to say, and I chuckled.

"Yeah, well, that's all that Daddy could get me."

She huffed. "Must be nice to have a dad who cares."

"Oh, don't mistake his *insistence* for concern for my comfort." The sarcasm dripped from my lips, but I didn't want to discuss my father with her.

She nodded, slightly rocking her body with the dip of her head. "You have a tent like a prince on safari," she teased with a touch of bitterness.

"You're the one with the condo tree house," I mocked, allowing the sudden irritation to take over my relief at seeing her on my beach.

"That's what you get when you have no one." This brought me up short and I looked directly at her—the curve of her nose, the sleek lines of her neck, and the slope of her shoulders.

"What do you mean *no one?*"

"What does *no one* typically mean?" she bit, rolling her neck to face me. Her eyes looked hollow, the irises too bright. I scooped my hand through the fine grains of sand to prevent me from touching her and looked away.

"That sucks," I muttered. As much as I hated my father and his intrusion into my life, I had to admit he'd been there for me. He provided me with a home. He paid for my education. We had food on our table. I didn't want for anything. I hadn't *wanted* until recently.

"I miss cookies," she said, startling me as if she could read my thoughts. I turned to look at her, observing once again the elegant curve of her neck, the angle of her shoulder, and the length of her fingers.

"I miss bourbon." The comment made me swallow. How I longed for the burn to take away the awkwardness between us. My eyes roamed her body.

"What are you wearing?" It occurred to me that she wasn't dressed like someone in confinement but like a girl lost in the woods. Cut off khaki shorts and a bright red tank top were not the adventurous outfit I expected. She looked like a pin-up wannabe with her perky breasts peeking out the top curve of her tank and long legs leaning out the short hem of her shorts. I swallowed at images of her I shouldn't have. "Why don't you have a bunch of safari shit or something?"

"Because I'm not on a safari. Or a vacation." She looked me up and down, taking note of my plaid colored board shorts. "And I don't have money for new clothes."

The thought stopped me. If she didn't have money for clothes, how was she paying for the necessities of this program? I'd been forced to pay my own way, even though this was a sanctioned punishment. I parted with my NCR Leggera 1200 street bike to cover expenses for this island.

"You're too skinny," I blurted.

"Is that supposed to insult me?" Her eyes flared, and the violet color of her eyes steamed to a deep purple.

"No, no, I just mean…do you have food? Is someone bringing you food?" I didn't know why I was stumbling through my words, but I wanted to know if she had enough to eat.

"I'm good," she muttered, letting her hands fall from her legs and digging her fingers in the sand like me.

"You look tired," I added.

"Wow, you're full of compliments today. Is that how you get the girls? Oh, right, I know how you get girls."

My eyes narrowed. "What's that supposed to mean?" I snapped, swiping a hand through my unruly hair.

Ignoring my temper shift, she spoke. "I can't sleep at night. Each time I close my eyes I imagine I hear another snake." She shivered next to me, and I wanted to wrap my arm around her shoulder and pull her close to me. She looked at me again, those purple eyes gleaming.

"You're turning into a bit of a grizzly," she said, deflecting the subject and biting the corner of her lip. I couldn't tell if she was trying to insult me in return.

"I can't see myself to shave."

She grinned. It was measured and tentative, but her lips curled and her face brightened just a little bit. She was pretty in a natural way, but I imagined she'd be beautiful if she fully smiled.

"What are you smiling about, Mouse?"

The fire died in her eyes, and she turned away from me.

"You think I'm weak, don't you?" She brushed her hands on the sides of her shorts then returned her palms to the sand to press upward. My hand shot out, encircling her too-thin wrist and stopping her movement to stand. Her skin was warm, burning under my palm. I didn't want her to go. Speaking with her had been the most conversation I'd had in weeks. Just the presence of another person was bringing me comfort, and I didn't want her to leave me on a negative note.

"Stay."

She gasped.

"You said you aren't sleeping. Stay here. I can…I can watch over you."

Her eyes opened wider, the violet color draining to a muted lavender.

"I mean, I can sleep outside the tent. I won't touch you." I released her wrist and held my hands up in surrender. She'd been crouched toward me with the force of my tugging on her wrist, but she straightened to stand.

"I can't stay here," she whispered, her voice catching as she spoke. Shaky fingers brushed loose hair behind her ear.

"Then why did you come here today?" I snapped, standing myself to face her. I stood a head taller than her tiny frame.

"I don't know," she growled, shaking her head as she looked off toward the bay again. The air hummed around us, the tension between us building. The animal in me wanted to hitch her over my shoulder and take her back to my tent. I wanted to force her to sleep. She looked dead on her feet, and I didn't like the fact she was unprotected, even fifteen feet in the air. Her face lifted toward me, and her eyes narrowed.

"I'm going back to my corner of the island." She crossed her arms, holding herself together like she'd done after the snake attack.

"Fine," I snarled.

"Fine," she said, brushing past me and disappearing once again into the thick brush.

# 13

# Day 28 – Juliet

I stomped back to my spot in the jungle, forcing each step like a child having a tantrum. It took more strength than he'd known to come to his beach and wait for him. I wanted to thank him for what he'd done to save me, but the moment he opened his mouth, I hated him again. I swatted at the foliage obscuring my hissy-fit as I trudged back to my space.

I reached for the rope ladder but paused as the world spun a little. Wiping my brow, I continued upward despite shaking hands. At one point, I slipped and slid my arms through the rung to hold myself steady. By the time I reached the platform, I was shaking from a cold sweat. Swiping my forehead again, I found I was warm to the touch and longed for a warm bath, even though I'd taken a cool one before I went to his tent.

I don't know why I bothered to clean myself for him. He wasn't important to me. I didn't care that he called me skinny or said I looked tired. I was tired. Climbing the rope ladder took all my strength with none remaining to pull up the rope ties. I wanted to prove to him I wasn't weak, but he'd called me *Mouse* again, and I despised the nickname.

I stretched for my bed and then curled onto my side. My teeth rattled slightly, and I pulled the blanket over myself, falling into a restless sleep.

++

I awoke on the dirt floor of the jungle, my head aching from resting on the root of a tree. I'd crawled down the ladder after the smell of my own waste got the better of me. There was no modern convenience of toilets and plumbing, and when the chamber pot was full enough to reek, I'd found my way to the base of the ladder, using the wild as a latrine. I hadn't made it far. My stomach lurched and I released from any opening, my body rejecting whatever had caused this fever. Convinced I was going to die, I curled up at the base of my tree, reveling in the coolness of the leaves and dirt beneath me. I don't know how long I lay in this position, but I believed I'd been here at least a day, maybe two. I didn't have the strength to stand. I hardly had the energy to crawl away to relieve myself. The stench lingered around me.

"Jesus, what is that smell?" The masculine tenor circulated somewhere above my head, and, sick as I was, I groaned at the possibility that he found me laying in waste and smelling like a sewer.

"Leave me alone," I mumbled, not certain the words left my lips.

"Juliet?" he questioned as if there could be any other female on the island. I didn't answer him. Footsteps crunched softly on the leaves nearby and a shadow fell over me. "Juliet!" The frantic tone surprised me.

"What happened?" Instantly, I sensed him kneeling before me, but I refused to open my eyes. *Go away*, I prayed, hoping he was a dream, an illusion I conjured in my misery. A cool hand cupped my cheek.

"You're burning up." The sound of his voice was too loud, and I winced. Feet scrambled near my head and I heard the clank of the rope ladder being jostled. *He's stealing everything from me*, I thought, and then decided I didn't care. He could take whatever he needed.

His presence returned. "Can you walk?" he asked but didn't wait for a reply before scooping me up and cradling me against his chest. The cool sensation of his cotton T-shirt under my cheek was a nice respite from the hardness of the ground.

"Don't…" I couldn't finish my thought. *Don't carry me.* I wanted to question where he was taking me, but I didn't have the strength to ask. He'd be able to do whatever he pleased to me. Disgusting as I was at the moment, he didn't seem repelled by me. We traveled what felt like an eternity before he set me on the ground again. Beneath my shirt and shorts, I was naked. I stopped bothering with a bra and underwear when the fever hit. Tack didn't remark on that fact as he removed my clothing and cradled me again, and I was too spent to care, as the sound of rushing water and the gentler sounds of lapping strides overtook my senses before he lowered me into the cool pool. I might have groaned at both the comfort and the ache. My body trembled.

"Shhh, I'm not going to hurt you," he said, and the words conjured all kinds of memories. With no will to fight him, I mumbled, "Just let me die."

He pulled me tighter to his chest, as we were both dipped into the water. He brushed a hand over my hair. The cool touch was a welcome sensation to my aching head.

"You're not going to die."

"I want to," I muttered. The pain in my skull made me want to lop off my own head. My stomach rumbled with the jostling of our walk. My body ached in places I didn't know could feel pain.

"Don't say that. I don't believe you. You wouldn't be on this godforsaken island searching for forgiveness if you wished to die. I don't want to hear that." His tone was sharp, and he jiggled me against him as if the force of physical pressure could rid me of the thoughts. I winced. I had nothing left. No one cared about me. The experiment was a failure with his presence. I had nothing to live for.

"Hold on," he demanded and I was lifted once again, my skin prickling from the loss of the cold water. My body shivered again in the heat. He shifted to place me on my feet but my legs gave out. I anticipated the hard ground but he caught me before I landed. "Shit," he mumbled before something encircled my body, soft and comforting like a sheet.

"Don't give up," he commanded, and my feet were swept out from under me. Wrapped in his arms again, he carried me once more. I had no idea where he was taking me, and I settled into the jolting motion as the world disappeared.

++

"Drink," he commanded.

Pressed to a sitting position, it was warm where I sat, too warm. Something cool pressed my lips and I opened without thought then clamped my mouth closed. I couldn't handle food. I didn't want to drink. I spit out the liquid, feeling something else behind my teeth.

"We're going to play this my way, Mouse," he said, and my throat closed. My tongue fought the pills behind my teeth. My heart raced and a memory flashed. Eyes shooting open, blinking in the dim light, I pushed back on the hand holding a spoon outstretched toward my lips. I swatted as if a bug buzzed near my head.

"Jesus, settle down," he snapped. Liquid trickled down the front of my shirt and a spoon hit the bedding.

"Oh no," he muttered. "Swallow it." A finger pressed on my lips until I couldn't hold back any longer. Invading my mouth, his finger forced the tablets to my throat. I bit down on the digit.

"Fuck, Mouse," he snapped, snatching his index finger from my mouth.

I pulled my head back, continuing to press my hands forward, but a firm hand held my neck. Panic set in. My feet began to kick at a sheet. The flat of my hand hit his bare chest. The other palm pressed out at his wrist, desperately pushing.

"Stop fighting me," he demanded and squeezed the nape of my neck. "It's fever medicine. Swallow it. And you need to try to drink something. Anything." There was a pause as his voice cracked. "Please."

I stilled, and my eyes shifted to him. His head bowed as he shook it side to side. His eyes were closed as if in frustration. I'd made a mess of myself, and the moisture seeped through my shirt. Lifting a weak hand, I tried to swipe at the spill on my chest with my knuckles. His head shot up, and he looked directly at my eyes.

"I'll get you another clean shirt." Releasing my neck, he scrambled off the pallet that held a mattress and an open sleeping bag. The sheet was at my feet and I looked down at myself. The motion made me dizzy, and I lay back. A down pillow caught my head, and I nuzzled into the comfort.

"I'm going to change you again," he stated, reaching for the hem of my shirt and beginning to lift the material. My hand swatted at his.

"I promise not to look, but you already showed me everything," he teased. I smacked at him again.

"I can do it," I choked.

"I'm trying to help." His voice rose, and I stopped struggling, letting my fingers come to rest on his wrist. It wasn't sensual, but it felt intimate as if my body shifted from fight to flight, and I held onto him to hold me steady, tethering me to the ground. We sat for the longest sixty seconds of my life with my hand clutching his wrist and his eyes staring into mine before I released him and sat up to dress myself. He had the decency to shift his body, and I slipped off the wet tee. Redressing took all my strength, and I lay on his pillow once more.

"You need to drink something. Just a little bit." I nodded, allowing him to hold up my head and swallowing a few sips of cold water. I pulled back too quickly, and water trickled down my chin to my neck. He took the shirt I'd just worn and wiped at my jaw, caressing my collarbone.

"Try to sleep again. I'll be right here."

That's what I was afraid of, but I fell into a deep sleep.

++

With the pressure of a hand on my hip, I woke with a start, sitting bolt upright. Twisting, I found Tack next to me on the mattress. His fingers clutched my hip with the movement of me sitting. I looked down at myself to see I wore a shirt I didn't recognize. Two sizes too big, it slid off my shoulder.

"Hey," his sleepy voice croaked, sounding strangely seductive. He cleared his throat and teased, "You wake." I stared down at him a moment, his expression casual as he lay with his rumpled hair spread on the pillow. When I turned away from him, he sat up, running a hand through his unruly locks. It had grown long in a month. His green eyes glowed despite the darkness. His facial hair looked jagged, hanging in chopped patches. My eyes stopped on his mouth.

"I should go," I said, but he raised a hand to stop me.

"Don't even start with that again." I blinked in confusion. "You've been muttering for me to let you die, and take you home, and everything in between. You aren't going anywhere."

My tongue felt heavy in my mouth, and I swallowed the bad taste.

"I'm so thirsty."

To my surprise, his face brightened, a full smile curling his lips. My brow pinched in question, but he ignored me and hopped over my outstretched legs. He returned to the bed quickly with a cup of fresh water.

"Drink slowly. We don't want you getting sick again." His smile lessened a little, but the curl to his lips remained teasing.

"You feeling better, baby?" His hand brushed over my head, and between the touch and the term of endearment, I pulled back.

"Sorry," he muttered. I raised the cup to my lips and took few more slow sips. The water was tepid but refreshing. My mouth still felt like a cat settled in it.

"Think you could eat something?"

I shook my head, flexing my legs, stiff from disuse but no longer aching from the fever. He removed the cup from my hand and crawled back over me. I looked toward the opening of the tent where darkness was falling behind the flap.

"Don't even think about it," he mumbled, lying down beside me, his hand resting on the base of my spine. "Lay back down."

On autopilot, I did as he said, twisting my body to face away from him. My back toward him, his hand returned to my hip.

"You were pretty sick. Are you sure that snake didn't get you?"

I shook my head as an answer.

"That was one of the scariest moments of my life," he mumbled, his breath brushing the back of my neck. My hair was clumped in a loose loop and tied with a band, but I didn't remember wrapping it. "But seeing you on the jungle floor, surrounded by…" His voice faded and I heard him swallow. "I thought that was it." His tone lowered. "I thought I'd lost you."

"Why were you there?" My own voice croaked from disuse.

"I felt bad about how things went when you came to the beach. I wanted to apologize for my attitude." We both seemed to suck in a breath at the admission. The words tumbled off his lips, but I felt him stiffen behind me as if he surprised himself with what he said.

"I'm sorry." The apology was so low, I wasn't sure I heard him. The hand at my hip slipped to my lower belly. It was my turn to stiffen in response, but he ignored the rigidity and tugged me to him. My back hit his chest and his hand climbed upward between my breasts. "I'm sorry," he whispered, a warm breath caressed my neck, tickling the hairs at the nape.

His hand continued its travels, coming to rest over my heart which raced fast enough I assumed he could feel it through the T-shirt I wore.

"I'm sorry," he said again, the presence of his lips on my neck sent a shiver down my skin. His palm flattened. Starting at his elbow, shaking fingers of my own traced up his arm. The tips of my fingers tickled through the fine curly hair of his forearm and came to rest over the back of his hand. He spread his fingers and I slipped mine between his. Clutching our fingers together, he tugged me even tighter into the embrace. A tear slipped from my eye and crept down my nose. It itched, but I didn't dare release his fingers, fisted with mine over my heart.

"I'm sorry," he whispered once more.

# 14

# Day 30 – Tack

I woke to the sound of a motor boat approaching. The engine had cut, and I propped up on an elbow. Looking down before me, I found Juliet still sleeping, clutching my hand in hers against her chest. Without thinking, I lowered to kiss her ear.

"Don't move."

Her breath hitched and her eyes popped open. She spun for me, and I moved quick enough so her face didn't collide with my nose.

"Garvey and Colton are here."

I released her hand and hopped over her body. She scrambled back at the same time, pressing herself against the tent corner.

"What is it?" I whispered, reaching for her. She pulled back her arm, shaking her head.

"Who are Garvey and Colton?"

"Garvey is my restoration coach. Colton is his son. They don't know you're here." She nodded in understanding but the glazed look in her eyes proved she didn't comprehend. "Look, let me get rid of them. Then I can explain everything. Just stay in the tent. Don't let them see you."

I fumbled as I stood, searching the floor of the tent for something to wear. I wasn't allowed to sleep away the days, and I had no sense of timing other than it must be near noon at the end of a month. My two-week supply visit had arrived.

I'd pulled on a fresh T-shirt and stepped toward the flap before stopping and turning back to face her.

"You okay, Mouse?" My forehead wrinkled in concern as I saw her tucked into the corner, the sheet pulled up to her neck. Her eyes, wide and glassy, stared back at me. I wanted to stalk back to the bed and assure her she had nothing to fear but I also didn't want to risk Garvey and Colton finding her here.

This was banishment, and the punishment included solitary confinement. I didn't want them to find I'd broken the rules. While I tried to convince them two weeks ago she existed, it had now come to a point that I didn't want to share her. I stepped through the tent entrance as Garvey and Colton each crossed the beach, a box in hand.

"You know, you could greet us and help carry your own supplies," Colton chirped.

"Yeah, well, you can fuck off," I muttered. From the moment I met Colton, he didn't care for me, and there was nothing I liked about him. Cocky, self-assured, but small town and wise-ass, I didn't appreciate the way he snubbed me. He clearly thought he was better than me although he had less to offer. I wanted to wipe the smirk off his face each time he looked at me as we sat in some stupid restorative circle, talking out the process of my consequences. A talking stick was passed, in the custom of the Native American culture, and at times, I wanted to shove that stick up his ass.

This day, I wanted him to leave as soon as possible. I relieved him of the box he carried and set it outside my tent. Quickly, I interceded Garvey and did the same. As with his prior visit, Garvey sat on a turned-up tree stump near the cooled fire pit.

"What have you done these last two weeks?" How could I tell them all I'd done? I'd fucked her, saved her, and cared for her. The last thought stopped me short. *I'd taken care of her*, I corrected. *I didn't care for her, did I?* I still disliked what she'd done to sentence us here on the island. But when I thought about it, it seemed strange that I no longer wanted to beg Garvey to get me out of here. I didn't want to speak of her. What I wanted was that hint of a smile I'd seen days ago. One moment she looked fierce and the next she looked frightened. I wanted to change that.

"I've read," I lied. "And I've written a little." Actually, I'd worked out quite a bit in between my interactions with Juliet. Colton eyed me in disbelief but Garvey nodded his head, the only hint he was pleased.

"Are you still angry?" Garvey asked and the question startled me.

"Of course, I'm still angry," I snapped, realizing too late, the question intended to trap me. The truth was, I wasn't as angry as I had been. I had done some soul searching, mainly about Rick and what kind of friend he had been. I couldn't say I was in his shadow, as we equally craved the limelight, but I'd come to realize he was always one step ahead of me in pushing the envelope. And he went too far with Juliet. I shuddered when I thought of him with her, the gleam in his eyes as he took her, the loss in hers as she felt his violation. I can't believe I watched, thinking it was something I wanted to do.

"You need to dance," Garvey broke into my thoughts.

"What?" I snorted.

"You need to become one with nature. Pick an animal. Reenact its behavior and reflect on what you can learn from it."

"I am not fucking dancing," I said aloud this time, adding a humorless chuckle.

"Suit yourself," Garvey said, slapping his thighs as he stood.

"Still hallucinating about the girl?" Colton mocked.

"I'm not arguing about the girl with you," I growled. Garvey's brows rose in response, and a small smile twitched his flat lips. A rustle from behind the bushes to my left brought Garvey and Colton's attention in that direction, providing an out for any further discussion of Juliet. My focus shifted back to the tent. My fists clenched when I heard a thump.

"What was that?" Colton asked, shifting his feet from the direction of the shore to my tent. I stepped before him, cutting off his path.

"I'm sure it was nothing."

"What are you hiding?" He narrowed his jet-black eyes on mine.

"Nothing." My voice caught as the bushes rustled again. Releasing my focus from Colton, he circled me and headed for my tent. A small flock of birds flew from the trees to our right, distracting us all and bringing relief as it offered an explanation for the movement in the foliage. Colton opened the flap to my tent, though, before I could reach him. He remained outside the entrance, peering inward. As I approached, I looked over his outstretched arm holding open the flap. My shoulders slumped in relief when I didn't see Juliet. There was no sign of her sickness as the bed was made tidy and neat. No article of her clothing remained on my floor. The cup of water didn't rest on the crate I used as a bed stand. I tensed with concern. *Where had she gone?*

# 15

# Day 30 – Juliet

I smiled at Lillian, hoping the tremble to my hands and the quake of my smile didn't alert her to anything. She'd already been concerned for my nutrition. I was beginning to worry about my sanity. Letting her know I'd had a jungle fever could end the experiment. One stipulation of the process was not to deprive me of modern amenities. There was no reason not to have a supply of acetaminophen for a fever or a headache. Tack must have found my stash, as that's what he forced down my throat in order to help me. The thought softened my forced smile as Lillian stood under my tree house.

"We missed you at the dock. Where were you?"

"I'd gone for a soak," I lied, realizing the most obvious sign would be wet hair, which I didn't have. Tack's too-large shirt hung off my shoulder, falling just above my knees. I smelled like him—man and sunscreen.

"Whose shirt is that?" Her eyes narrowed and a thin-lined smile crossed her lips.

"My uncle's," I said, too quickly. Lillian knew me well enough to know I'd own nothing of his. I didn't even want to see him at the hearing or the restorative trial, but I had to have a family member present as a witness to my acceptance of the program. I didn't want him there any more than he wanted to be there, but as my only living relative, he fit the need. If I died, I needed a family member to claim the body. I laughed at that stipulation in the contract. He'd rather let me rot than collect me.

Her eyes questioned my response but refocused on my face.

"You look thin." It wasn't said as an insult, nor a compliment. Lillian was concerned. She knew I'd stopped eating after what happened. Starving myself was a sign of depression, and she worried at moments that the experiment was too much. As excited as she was to promote my case to the restorative circle, she was equally nervous I would relapse once I was alone. As I wasn't alone, there wasn't much chance of relapsing.

"I've been a little under the weather," I said, trying to assure her with a larger smile that all was well presently. Telling her about Tack was on the tip of my tongue. The information clawed behind my teeth. I had so many questions, so many emotions. I was confused by his attention to my illness, grateful for his rescue from the snake, but I still feared he'd retaliate against me. Rick had. Why wouldn't Tack?

One thing I'd noticed about Tack, despite his sense of entitlement and I'm-better-than-the-world air, was a sadness to his eyes, and a touch of panic. He didn't like to be alone, but he didn't trust himself to admit it. I wanted to believe his apology last night was deeper than simply saying he was sorry for forcing me to swallow pain medicine and demand I sleep next to him. However, I couldn't be certain. I didn't trust him.

"Do you need to leave?" Lillian asked. "We could rethink your sentence."

"No," I answered too quickly. I'd been found guilty of involuntary manslaughter. Ironically, Brandon came to my defense, exposing what he'd seen as my reaction at the bar. He'd walked in on Rick reaching for me, after asking if I liked what he'd done. When I stabbed him, Brandon immediately said it was self-defense, and I was convicted of the lesser offense.

"That's what I'm going to say," he whispered, as he called the police while blood trickled down my arm. While I hadn't planned to go in the bar and kill Rick that day, nothing stopped me from reacting to his presence—his nearness alone was a threat to my being. The tape mysteriously appeared during the trial, and the men were exposed. The defense wanted to prove I had the intent to kill. The prosecutor proved the tape showed a previous crime had gone unpunished. Two men were visible on the tape. The rest didn't get their turn. Brandon's interruption to that initiation party lasted long enough to distract Rick and deflate the intention of the gathering. I'd dulled my thoughts by then, resigned to what was happening.

My body rippled, releasing the thought, chilled despite the heat. A fever could linger or spike again, and suddenly, I was exhausted. Lillian eyed me suspiciously.

"Is everything okay here? Do you feel safe?" I found the questioning odd, considering Lillian assured me it was safe to be here. I nodded in answer. For some reason, I didn't feel threatened. After all that Tack had done for me, taking care of me, I wasn't ready to leave. Strangely, I felt protected on the island. Lillian was giving me an out, but I wanted to keep going with the experiment. I wanted to know where the island would lead me.

"I'm fine, just tired and a little shaky." My fingers did tremble as I held them out for Lillian to see.

"Your tree house looked like a small disaster." Lillian smiled, comforting me with her concern. "Franco and I cleaned it up. Let's get you back to bed. I want to exam you myself." With a tender hand, she reached out for my shoulder, prodding me toward the ladder and I followed her, allowing her to mother me.

++

Lillian decided to spend the night. The driver of her boat, Franco, camped under the tree house while she perched in a seat next to my bed. She sponged down my body and gave me more fever reducers. She made me warm broth and fed me. At moments, tears came to my eyes, remembering my own mother doing the same thing when I was sick as a child. Then I thought of Tack and his attempts to make me drink water from a spoon. I smiled slightly at the thought.

"Pleasant dreams," Lillian asked, staring at me. "You drifted off for a moment. Where did you go?" Again, the desire to tell her about Tack and how different he was from the man at the club fought within my mouth for release. I didn't want to be fooled, though. Tack from the island and Tack of The Front Door were still the same person.

"Just remembering my mother," I said softly. Lillian smiled, her blue eyes sparkling with kindness and sympathy.

"My mother called life an adventure," she said. "She taught me to explore everything. And everyone." She chuckled as she winked. I'd heard these things before from Lillian. While my idol was Margaret Meade, hers was her mother, another famous anthropologist who studied urban life instead of the lives of the Samoans. Both women were before their time, with open ideas about sexuality and the role of women.

"I've been doing some self-exploration." I had been doing some deep soul-searching. *Was I angry at Rick or myself?* In many ways, there was no excuse for a man like Rick Fontaine, but I was angry with myself for being in a position to be captured like I was. Women are taught to never take the blame. No means no, and it does, unequivocally. But all my life, I'd been cautious of men and aware of my surroundings. My guard was down that night, and I knew why I was distracted.

"Sometimes the things we learn about others come from looking at ourselves as individuals first," Lillian said, patting my arm. The touch soothed me, and I smiled more genuinely at her words of wisdom. I admired her and appreciated her help with my case.

"Get some rest, honey," she said, but I'd slept enough lately. It was time for me to wake up and take charge of my life again. I needed to finish my sentence on this island and get back to reality.

# 16

# Day 33 – Tack

"Thank fuck," I muttered as I crossed over the rocky ledge and found her wading in the pond below. She walked under the waterfall, disappearing for a moment, before returning to stand under the cascade. Brushing back her hair, her face rose to the filtered sunshine streaming through the trees. Just seeing her move without measured steps made my heart skip a beat.

The water was only waist deep, exposing her breasts to me. The globes ripe and peaked at the nipple made my mouth water. I reached for my shoes and began undressing. Her eyes opened, sensing my hungry leer on her. Blood raced through my veins, the naked look of her becoming an addiction to me. She lowered into the water, watching me, meeting my stare. Hastily undressing down to my boxer briefs, I stepped gingerly down the remainder of the rocks and entered the pond.

"Holy fuck! It's cold!" I shrieked, noticing her eyes playfully gleam in the reflection of the sun. "How do you handle this?" I continued to lower myself incrementally, worrying my dick might shrivel and freeze from the frigid water.

"You get used to it," she replied, swishing her arms through the water, sending ripples around her shoulders as she crouched in the protection of the pond.

I lowered deeper, taking full breaths to release the chilled tremor rippling up my body. Dipping to my waist, I bent at the knees and disappeared under the water. The cold shock took my breath, and I pressed upward, breaking the surface to find she stood close to me. I shook out my hair and she giggled. The sound stopped me. My lips curled in response. The din was sweet, and my body revived under the cool liquid. I mimicked her position, letting the water lap at my shoulders, arms outstretched to cause a subtle wake.

"How are you feeling?" I asked, noticing the faint purple under her eyes was not as prominent as it had been.

"Much better, thank you." She bit her lip, as if holding back a smile, and it forced another one from me. Pre-pubescent feelings of giddy awkwardness filled me, and I couldn't take my eyes from her. We stared at one another for a moment before a question that had been burning inside me had to be asked.

"I came to see you, but I saw someone sleeping under your tree house. Who was he?" The actual question came out harsh, a surge of jealousy nipping through my veins. Strangely, I didn't like the idea of another man looking after her.

"That's Franco, Lillian's driver." She paused, and I waited, tweaking an eyebrow to suggest I wanted more details. "Lillian is my academic advisor and restoration guardian."

The title brought me up short. *Was she not of legal age?* She looked young, but not that young.

"How old are you?"

"Twenty-five," she offered, looking over her shoulders as her arms gently pushed the water around her. I nodded in understanding.

"Garvey is my restoration coach. He and his son, Colton, come for my regular fifteen-day visit. I'm twenty-seven, by the way."

We were silent a second, water lapping between us. I noticed we were closer to one another than when I initially entered the pond.

"You didn't tell them about me?" she asked, and I shook my head. Her eyes shifted to the rocky side of the pond. "I see." She paused. "Why not?" The quietness with which she asked caught my breath. Did she think I was hiding her? Keeping her a secret?

"I don't want to share you with them," I said without thinking, offering more than I had admitted to myself lately.

"You did…" she stopped. Was she going to throw it in my face that I'd shared her before? The words would have stung, and I deserved the slap. I stepped closer to her.

"Not like that," I said.

"I didn't mean…" she faltered again.

"You did," I sighed, wiping a wet hand through my hair. "Anyway, what about you? Does this Lillian know about me? What about Franco?" I exaggerated his name, hinting at my jealousy. From his propped position under the tree, I could see he was a large man, meant for clearing jungles and wrestling alligators.

She smiled slowly, and my breath hitched. She was so pretty. "No. I didn't tell them about you either." While I wanted to ask her, *why not*, I didn't care about the answer.

We tread close enough to one another that our arms could no longer extend before us without bumping into one another.

"Tell me more about Lillian. You said, academic advisor. Are you a student?"

"I'm studying to be an anthropologist. I'm working on my Master's degree. Or I was...until..." The unspoken information hung between us. "Anyway, Lillian thought this situation would be good for field study. As well as reflective for me."

I nodded in understanding.

"I work for our family company. Corbin Industries couldn't have a mark against their name, though. My dad learned of this retributive process and decided it would be good for me. *You're too entitled*, he says." Sarcasm spat as I repeated my father's words, but she burst into laughter. A trill sound echoed off the rocks and surrounded us.

"You think that's funny, huh?" I reached out to playfully dunk her and then decided against it. My fingers brushed through her hair, cupping the locks behind her ear. Her laughter faltered, and her eyes widened. Our faces were less than a few inches from one another. Our knees brushed under the water.

"Tell me more about Lillian. Or your family? You mentioned you had no one. What happened?" Her eyes saddened before she spoke.

"My parents died when I was in eighth grade. I spent my high school years living with my uncle. It wasn't easy, and I worked hard to go to college."

"What wasn't easy, living with him or working hard?"

"Both." Her eyes lowered, and my fingertips came to her chin. I could see she didn't trust me with more information.

"Why were you at The Front Door?" This question confirmed any doubt I had of her trust. Her lips clamped and the motion physically told me she would not speak. I let the question slide and tried to offer my own history.

"I think things came too easily for me. I had anything I could ever want, which left me without knowing what I needed." Her eyes squinted at me. "Sometimes it isn't easy being at the top, either."

She scoffed.

"I'm serious. Nothing I did was good enough for my father. Under his pressure, I rebelled. Whatever I could do, I did. And I got away with most of it. He didn't stop me. He never stopped me." I shook my head and looked off in the distance.

"And what you wanted was someone to stop you?"

I shrugged my shoulder. I didn't know what I wanted. "In some ways, I thrived on the attention I received because I didn't receive it otherwise. School was too easy. Athletics like a second nature. When I obtained my first merger, I crushed it into pieces because of the owner's weakness." I smacked the water.

"Sounds like it *was* easy."

"But don't you see, all I did was take, because it was easy. No one fought me. Nothing was…difficult."

"Until now," she said, her voice lowered. I nodded.

"I wanted someone to give me permission, instead of always feeling like I could take whatever I wanted."

My eyes shifted downward, and I could see the sharp tips of her nipples beneath the water line. Her hands had disappeared. We seemed to be circling each other as we spoke.

"Sometimes, I think I'm dreaming you." My voice was low, as I stroked the hair over her ear again, focusing my eyes on the motion. I couldn't look her in the eyes as I spoke such things. Vulnerable to that violet glare, I was afraid she wouldn't believe me.

"I don't want you to be a dream," I muttered, a rugged timbre coming from my throat. We were even closer to one another, and her knees somehow came between mine. I no longer felt the cold liquid surrounding me, but warm heat radiating off her as I touched her. My knuckles skimmed down the side of her neck and lingered to her shoulder. A ripple of water caught the attention of my dick. I was hardening, despite the cold. I continued to gently rub a path from her shoulder, up her neck to her ear and back.

"Are you touching yourself?"

She gasped, shaking her head, but her face shaded a slight pink, and my lips twitched. My knuckles retreated below the water line, drawing close to the exposed swell of her breasts. Her chest rose and fell, but she hadn't uttered a sound. Her eyes remained on mine. I opened my hand to let my fingers tickle her skin. I could feel her heart race, and I took the risk to lower my fingertips and grace the slope of one breast. I stopped at the nipple and circled the tip. Her breath caught.

"Do you like that?" I asked, and she pulled back from my touch. Her brow pinched, as she pushed further away.

"What? What did I say?" Her expression troubled me. I didn't understand. "Tell me."

"That's…that's what *he* asked me…"

My hand reached for her arm, preventing her retreat. "I don't want you to think of him when you're with me."

She gasped again. "Then you shouldn't have been there with him. Your presence and his memory tangle together too often in my head."

I sighed, exhaling deeply, releasing my hand from her arm and holding it up in surrender.

"I'm sorry. You're right." My voice lowered, and my eyes fell in shame. I shouldn't have been there. I knew why I was, and I knew what I did, and neither thought made it easy to face her, especially when she blatantly reminded me.

"Help me," I stressed as I reached for each of her shoulders, unable to deny myself from touching her. My thumbs caressed gently over her smooth, cool skin. "How can I make it better?" I begged. My eyes raced back and forth, uncertain where to focus but desperate with need for her assistance to make things right for her. She tugged back, settling into the water to release my touch. We stared at one another a moment, my eyes willing her to tell me something, *anything*.

"I just...I find there are triggers for me. Things that are said. Phrases. It brings back a memory." My finger reached for her hair and scooped around her ear. I wanted to draw her close and hold her against me. I wanted her to forgive me.

"Is there a way to stop me before I say one?" I asked.

She chuckled softly. "I don't think so."

"I'm—*not*—Rick," I uttered forcefully, my chest rising with the declaration. "I am not like him."

"Prove it." I paused, thinking for a moment, willing my thoughts to conjure a way to show her I was different in so many ways from who Rick was and who I'd been.

"Can I ask something instead?"

Her eyes squinted in question, her head tilting to the side in suspicion.

"I'm asking permission," I clarified, but I didn't know how I'd respond if she denied me. My fingers began to shake along her neck. My voice came out meek as I asked, "May I kiss you?"

We stared at one another a moment as her eyes widened. She looked away as if to process the question, collecting her own thoughts. Then she spun back to face me.

"Just one," she whispered. I stared back at her. She remembered me asking, pleading for one kiss *that* night. I could have taken anything I wanted from her, but her lips were what I needed. One kiss to let me know what we were doing was okay with her. And when she refused, I knew it wasn't.

She stood before me, half her body exposed above the water, and I blinked up at her in surprise. I stood slowly to match her height. Time seemed to slow. My breaths increased. My hand stilled on her neck and her throat rolled under my touch as she swallowed.

"Just one," she repeated, so low I could have mistaken it for the rush of the waterfall. Only I no longer heard the sound of the descending water behind her, as all my attention was aimed at her mouth. And then my lips descended to hers.

# 17

# Day 33 – Juliet

He was kissing me. Soft lips brushed mine, hesitant and gentle. The tip of his tongue skimmed my lips, and I sighed. The sound gave him permission, and he increased the pressure. Sucking at tender skin, he pulled at my lips with his, and I responded, surprising myself. His hand remained at my throat, and our knees knocked under water, but his mouth had all my attention. His tongue lapped at the seam of my mouth, and I opened for him. We moved in unison, our feet easily touching the bottom of the pond. The water only waist high, which meant the instant we stood my swollen breasts hit his cool chest. My hands came to his shoulders but he didn't tug me any closer to him.

He kissed me.

Mouths moved in opposing rhythm that cut a pattern of nipping and licking. The tempo increased, and I felt a familiar ache tremble low in my belly. I clenched my thighs, and a new beat struck, the pulse rapidly filling me. My mouth became more curious, my tongue seeking his. I stroked over it, purring gently as he returned the curiosity by invading my mouth. His lips tugged at mine, drinking me in, and then I was released.

I panted after the abrupt stop. His eyes focused on mine.

"You're turned on." It was a question and a surprise. How could he not see what he'd done to me? He'd done it before. My body vibrated with need. Either he'd have to touch me, which I wasn't ready for, or I needed to be excused to relieve myself.

Gentle fingers skated down my throat and traced along my collar bone from side to side. His eyes followed the trail of his fingers. Slowly, they lowered, seeking the swell of each breast, rounding over one and dipping to circle the other. My breathing increased and my chest rose, nearly begging him to touch me. His eyes pulled up to mine, seeking permission for something I wasn't able to handle yet. Rethinking the infinity symbol he drew around and between my breasts, he moved in another direction. A single fingertip stroked down the slope of one breast to touch my nipple as he'd done under the water.

"You're perfect," he whispered, letting his eyes drift to where he touched. "I want so much more of you, but I'm afraid to ask. Afraid I won't stop myself. Let me watch you."

I understood his meaning, and my hand slipped over my stomach. His eyes focused lower while his finger traced tantalizing circles over my nipple, occasionally pinching the tight bud. He watched as my fingers disappeared, but he knew I stroked through slick folds. The pressure built quickly, and as his fingertip increased, the repetition of my touch did as well.

His other hand slipped into his soaked boxer briefs. The sodden clothing accentuated the thick length of him, the white material nearly opaque from the water. He fisted himself. The subtle slick sound of skin stroking skin filtered through the air. The water lapped at his thighs, as he was taller than me.

"May I ask—" he whispered, and I reached for him without him completing the question. It was bold to touch him, sliding my hand into his underwear and gripping him. He let out a heavy groan, a sound that rolled from the depths of his throat but spoke of pleasure. I smoothed my palm over his mushroomed head and then wrapped my fingers around the silky, smooth shaft. It was a bit awkward, working within his wet underwear, and I fumbled slightly with my rhythm, but when I saw his eyes roll back momentarily, I felt empowered. This is what he wanted. He wanted permission. This is what I needed. I needed to feel in control. His sounds and his movements proved I had it over him.

*The power rests in me.*

I squeezed him tighter, producing a hiss from his lips and a milky substance at the tip. The sight made me gasp, and I panted as the flutter inside me increased.

"Yes. Like that, Mouse." The nickname should have stopped me, but it only pissed me off. This heightened the stroking of myself and the friction on the length of him. His hand covered mine, and he worked us in tandem to get where he needed. With fingers still on my nipple, he pinched me hard. "Now, baby," he grunted. Watching him ejaculate on my fist set me over the edge. I cried out, rocking over my hand. His hand slipped to my hip, squeezing me to keep up the rhythm, but I'd had enough. Exhausted, I let go of him and withdrew my hand from between my legs. I sank into the water and pressed back from him. He stared down at me, slowly smiling, green-eyes gleaming. Unabashed that he stood before me, partially peeking out the band of his underwear, he ran a hand through his hair.

"Have dinner with me," he said, and I blinked up at him.

I turned for the rocks to exit the pond. His eyes weighed on my back as I climbed out of the cold water. I didn't look back, but I wanted to see the expression on his face. Not only had he never asked for things, I sensed he'd never been told no. I only had one way to compromise.

"Maybe."

# 18

# Day 33 – Tack

Crouching by the grill over the fire pit, I flipped the steak Garvey had brought me.

"You survived one month. Treat it as a celebration, make it a feast." He explained to me on his last visit how food was more than a necessity. He told me about one time he divided a hot dog into two halves for a previous student. The former ate his portion in two bites, and Garvey asked him how it tasted. The student commented that the hot dog was food, perfunctory. It tasted like the layer of ketchup he dumped over his section.

"He wanted it, so he ate it," Garvey explained. With hand motions, he pantomimed how he sprinkled his with celery salt and added onions. He exaggerated the motions of swirling mustard on top and pressing a slice of tomato between the bun and delicacy. Then Garvey opened wide and pretended to bite. He moaned.

"I explained to him that my portion was a celebration. I seasoned the hot dog to my liking, taking pleasure in the preparation. I thanked the Creator for providing such good offerings and savored the treat. I made it a feast, and I shared it with him. You need to learn to do the same thing."

I'd thought about what he said, knowing this was one more of Garvey's roundabout lessons. I drank and I ate and I fucked. I'd made them all something I wanted instead of something I appreciated. The motions had become automatic, and I did them because that's what I did.

But tonight, I hoped to change all that, starting with this steak. I flipped it again, attempting not to burn it. The flames were hot in the heat of the evening, and sweat trickled down the side of my face. I'd found a very wrinkled, white linen shirt and some semi-clean army-green shorts to wear. Rolling the sleeves past my elbows, the shirt was still too warm for the tropical heat, but I wanted to look decent in the foolish hope she'd join me. I stared at the flames, praying to whoever might listen that she would appear.

Movement to the right caught my attention, and I glanced in that direction. I turned back to the steak and then took a second look. Standing just outside the tree line stood a vision in white. Her hair hung in waves, tucked behind each ear. I'd never seen it down, other than saturated by the pond. The dress she wore was strapless, puckered in a way that accentuated the straight cut across her breasts. The remainder flowed loosely to her ankles. The material was filmy, and I could see through it, noting that she wore bikini underwear underneath. I blinked as I stood, willing her to not be a mirage, but rather some island goddess come to enlighten me.

As she stepped closer, I saw her fists clench at her sides. She was nervous, and suddenly so was I.

"You look beautiful," I said, exhaling a breath. She'd taken mine away again when she bit the corner of her lip fighting that smile I desperately wanted to see. Her hands clutched the side of her dress and she pulled it out a little, fanning the material to flutter in the breeze.

"It seemed silly to pack a dress, but my mother taught me at an early age never to go anywhere without at least one." She let the material fall and looked up at me. Violet eyes took my breath again and I sucked in air. I couldn't speak.

"It smells delicious," she said, nodding toward the steak and I noticed the extreme flame.

"Shit." I knelt immediately and slid the steak to the side of the grill grate. I wanted everything to be perfect and suddenly I was messing this up like an amateur. I wanted wine and flowers, damning Garvey for his feast lecture. And then realized, I didn't need them. I only wanted her company. We'd make do.

I lived in a luscious wilderness of flowers and noting a white bloom on the tree next to my tent, I walked over to the bush. Plucking the flower, I returned to Juliet holding it out to her.

"I should have gathered more." We both looked at the star-shaped petals before gazing up at each other. Her smile broke, and the brilliance was greater than the sun. In that moment, I decided I could live off that smile.

"It's perfect."

*You are*, I wanted to tell her again, but I'd already been enough of a sap. Instead, I tucked the flower behind her ear. Her lips curled and I longed to kiss her, but one thing at a time.

"I think this is almost ready," I said, stepping back to the steak and squatting to flip the meat one last time. "I'm sorry they only brought me one."

"I don't want to take your food," she said, her expression dropping.

"No," I said, standing. "No, I don't mean that way. I want to share it with you." I rubbed up her bare arm, taking the risk to touch her without asking. My body hummed with the simplest connection to her. Motioning for her to take a seat, I set to work removing the steak, cutting it in half and offering her a portion. I'd made rice in a pot, but it didn't look quite right, the consistency runny.

"I think I messed this up." Stretching from her log seat to look at the mushy mess, she giggled. "Yeah, I don't think that's quite right. It's okay. I had a bad maggot experience the first week here and I don't think I could stomach rice." I grimaced in response.

"No rice then."

I handed her a cup of water and raised mine.

"To one month on the island."

"To one month on the island," she replied before bringing the cup to her lips. We sat in silence a few minutes, slowly eating the rich food that had become an anomaly to both of us. I assumed her diet was similar to mine—canned goods and fruit.

"I feel like I want to ask you everything and don't know where to start," I chuckled, feeling awkward in a way I never had before.

"What do you want to know?"

"Anything you want to tell me." And so, our conversation began. A real conversation, where she told me about where she grew up and how it all changed when her parents died. She only gave me bits and pieces of her trailer park days, skipping ahead to meeting Chellie Brightson and attending college in Baltimore.

"It's how I ended up at The Front Door. The pay was good, and I needed the income to supplement my scholarship."

Suddenly self-conscious of my upbringing, I hesitated, but her eyes encouraged me to speak. Mentioning The Front Door closed the door on her history, so I began.

"I went to Georgetown. I thought I'd major in political science, but my father wanted me to join the family business. Corbin Industries owns a shipping yard in Virginia. We've begun to merge with other modes of transportation—trucking and railway. That's my job. Buying up smaller companies and adding them to our dynasty." The words took a sarcastic twist, and my lips followed the bitterness of my tone.

"And you like doing those things?" she questioned, interrupting my thoughts of the latest acquisition. I'd come to Baltimore and decided to hang with Rick. I'd heard of his club and wanted exclusive rights. He'd told me I could have what was his, but I knew Rick. I had to prove myself to him. *Enter Juliet.*

"I can be a bad man when I go into business mode. I tend to dominate until I get what I want. I want what I want, and that means taking companies, making them mine, and stripping them of what I need. My father always believed in survival of the fittest. He demands Corbin Industries be at the top."

"Have you ever considered doing something different? Building something up instead of tearing those companies down? Making something that's for the good of others?"

"No," I replied too sharply.

She smiled weakly, and I didn't like the turn of our conversation. My father was a ruthless man and I wouldn't have all that I had if he hadn't been. I wouldn't be who I was, ruthless myself, without his instruction. But then again, I wouldn't have done what I did, without thinking I could get away with it, because of who I was—Terrence Jackson Corbin *the fourth.*

"So why anthropology?" I questioned, deflecting the conversation from my father and the company.

"I've always been curious about people. People who are different from me. People who think like me but outside of my upbringing." She shrugged. "It's hard to explain."

"So why aren't you a shrink?" I chuckled, but her violet eyes pinned me.

"Because I don't want to dissect one person; I want to understand a whole culture." The comment made me pause.

"What culture?" The question caused her to open her mouth and then pause. Somehow, I felt we'd circled back to The Front Door, and my curiosity was piqued.

"Did you want to know more about what happened on the third floor?" I asked, hesitantly.

"Not so much that particular floor but a culture of people, a lifestyle. I didn't understand the desire to be dominated or submissive, for that fact. I want to be in control of my own life and decisions, but in some ways, I'm intrigued. Are submissives really subservient or do they have the dominating power? Aren't they in control after all—safe words and that sort of thing?"

"Uh…" *Fuck.* How did this conversation get to this? "Did you want to be a part of that?"

"I want to understand the mentality behind it." I stared at her. This waif of a woman, who had more strength than I'd witnessed in some men, and she was curious about this.

"Why?"

"Because I—" She stopped.

"Tell me. *I* want to understand." I'd set down my plate and leaned back against the stump at my back. I'd chosen the sand for a seat. Feeling satisfied with my feast and her company, this conversation was the most stimulating I'd had in months, even before the isolation of the island.

"I'm curious if the woman really is satisfied. Does the dominant actually care for her, or does he care *about* her? And how can he keep his emotions separate? How does she? I don't see how it's possible. I want to be in control of my life at all times but I'd love for someone to—" She stopped again, her eyes opening wide as she realized she was about to reveal too much. I sat on the edge of my proverbial seat, anxiously awaiting more. My palms dampened, and my mouth dried. *Did she want to be controlled?*

"You'd love what?" My voice harshly barked.

"I'd love someone to care for me. *About* me." She sighed as she shrugged, letting her eyes drop to her plate. My heart did a strange flip of relief. I didn't want her to be dominated by another. I wanted her to feel safe, confident, capable. She could do these things for herself, but I sensed her hesitation. She didn't believe in herself, and somehow, I felt I was to fault.

I noticed she hadn't eaten all of her steak, and I was concerned I'd burnt it too much. But more than the taste of the food, I worried we'd crossed a line that took her too deep into sharing with me. The air felt heavy between us, and I needed to change the subject.

"There's something I'd like to ask you."

Her head shot up in surprise, and as much as I wanted to beg her to submit to me so I could show her all the ways she could be cared for, I had other plans.

"Could you give me a haircut and shave?"

"What?" She laughed.

"I can't stand all this." I grabbed the hair on the top of my head. "And I'm certain I look like I have mange." I didn't own a mirror but tried to use the water to reflect my image. I had splotchy pieces of hair here and there that I could feel but never quite cut.

"I guess," she giggled again. I stood, went to my tent, and returned with a sharp, straight-edged razor and a shaving mug with soap. She eyed the razor held out to her, aware of the pain she could inflict with it. She'd wanted to kill me one night. I jostled the blade to break her attention.

"I trust you."

# 19

# Day 33 – Juliet

My hands shook as I took the blade from him. He sat on the stump seat and offered me the mug with soap. Holding the mug, he poured water over the shaving soap. He lathered his own jaw, and I stared at the motion. His cheeks filled with thick suds. Holding the brush, he flicked the remaining soap away from us.

"Stand behind me. Work the blade against the grain, like shaving your legs." I chuckled as it had been a while since I did that. Today had been the first time in a week. I walked behind him and tipped his head by cupping his chin to rest against my belly. His green eyes looked up at me as the blade rose to his neck. Quickly his hand rose and stopped my wrist.

"I trust you," he said again, then pulled my wrist to his lips and pressed a kiss over my pulse point. He closed his eyes, and with shaky hands, I began to slide the blade over his skin. The gritty sound echoed in the stilling evening. Once the first strip was complete, without nicking him, I continued in a steady pattern of cleaning the blade and shaving his jaw. His eyes remained closed, a peaceful look on his face. For a moment, I thought he'd fallen asleep.

"Finished," I whispered after a long silence. His lids opened slowly, revealing the deep moss color that narrowed in on me. My heart skipped a beat with the longing in them. He reached for a towel he'd set to the side of him and wiped the excess soap from his face.

"How do I look?" he asked, and I swallowed my reply. He was gorgeous. Cut from clay, and molded to perfection, his cheeks were accentuated by narrow bones and an edgy jaw line. He had a subtle tan line, his skin appearing to easily brown.

"You look good," I said, attempting to hold my voice steady. He looked almost as clean cut as he looked on *that* night.

"Hair next? I don't have scissors, so you'll have to just hack at it with the blade."

I laughed. "I can't do that. I've never cut hair. I don't want to mess it up."

"Anything is better than this mess," he said, gripping his hair in his hand. I did the best I could, razor-cutting off long strips of his hair and letting it fall at my feet. The process was daunting as I hacked at locks surprisingly silky despite our rugged conditions. The tips were sunbleached, and the removal of them restored him to his rich, brown color. It was choppy looking, but he rustled his hand through the strands, leaving it to lay as it fell in a fashionably messy way. The grizzly man was gone with this cut, but he didn't match the polished man he'd previously been. A stylish boy remained.

"How am I now?" he asked. I sensed the inquiry dug deeper than his appearance. He looked amazing, but the cutting of his hair softened his features. He looked less edgy and more wholesome. I smiled slightly at the change.

"You still look good," I teased.

"So do you," he replied, letting his eyes drip down my body. He quickly recovered, though, collecting his hair cuttings and adding them to the fire.

"I think I missed a spot," I said, noticing a clump in the back. He sat before me again, and I fixed it. "Better," I stated and ran my hands through his hair, mussing it up and shivering at the touch as it tickled my hand.

"You did good, Mouse."

The nickname dropped the smile from my face, and his eyes snapped open.

"What? Tell me that's not a trigger," he pleaded.

"I don't like that nickname."

"Why not?"

I turned away from him, setting the blade on another stump. "Thank you for dinner."

"Juliet, what did I say?" His eyes questioned mine.

"Actually, I hate that name," I clarified, blowing out a breath. His hands came to my shoulders, stroking down my arms to encircle my fingers.

"It suits you. A mouse might be small, but it's a brave creature, and resilient," he said, tugging me to him with our entwined fingers. "A mouse can scare an elephant, save a lion, squeeze through a hole the size of a pencil."

I chuckled. "I don't think the last one is a compliment." My breasts collided with his chest, and I was hyper-aware of us touching in such a manner.

"You and your compliments," he teased, kissing my forehead. "Come sit by the fire awhile."

He led me by our interlaced fingers.

"It's getting late," I pouted. The sky was turning a midnight blue, and although I'd braved the darkness of the jungle on several occasions, I didn't wish to do it that night. However, I said the opposite of my feelings. "I should go."

"It's too dark without you," he said, too briefly brushing his lips over mine. My mouth hungered for more, but words choked my tongue. The tone of his voice suggested darkness involved more than the midnight sky. He tugged me until he plopped to the ground, propping up against a log. He pulled me to sit between his spread knees, positioning me so I leaned back on his chest. We stared into the flickering flames.

"You're so far away if you go," he added, kissing my hair. I twisted to look up at him, questioning his tenderness. His words were sweet but unnerving. He couldn't possibly mean them. His fingers intertwined with mine, stroking over my knuckles and tickling inside my palms.

"You're saying that because I'm the only girl on the island," I blurted, adding laughter to soften the words that tasted bitter.

"What do you mean?" he whispered to the shell of my ear. My skin prickled at the soft brush of his lips.

"I'm the only female here, that's why you're attracted to me." Attracted might have been too strong a word. Interested, maybe? Intrigued? My comment startled him, and he pulled back.

"Why would you say that, Mouse?" His voice lowered as he said the nickname like a term of endearment, seductively sliding off his tongue. He stared at me. He was such a sexual being, and I was the only available person to satisfy his urges. However, I didn't wish to debate him when he tightened his hold on me. I remained quiet, and the minutes passed in strangely companionable silence.

"Thank you for sharing a feast with me," he softly said, pressing me against his chest again and resting his chin on my shoulder.

"A feast," I chuckled, not disappointed with the meal.

"Garvey says each meal should serve more than the purpose of obtaining food. It should be a celebration, and it should be shared. I was happy to celebrate with you. I want to share things with you." He was smooth, I thought, as my lips curled at the sweet words. Pensive for a moment, I tried to digest their meaning.

"Come into the tent with me." The gentle command tainted the sugary flavor of what he just said.

"I can't sleep with you," I blurted, sitting forward and twisting to face him.

"Just sleep," he said, his thumb caressing my knuckles. "Just sleep," he said lower. "I want to hold you." We stared at one another a moment before I settled back against him, my side on his chest, puzzled by the longing in his tone. He brushed my hair back from my face and neck. Rubbing circles on my back, he kissed my head again. Between the growing night, the warm fire, and the comfort of the man under my side, I drifted off into a restless sleep.

# 20

# Day 34 – Tack

At some point, she slept and I eventually carried her into my tent. She nuzzled against me, and I couldn't stop my lips from continually kissing her. Her hair. Her cheek. Her fingers. I laid her on my pallet and removed her sandals. I slipped off my shirt and climbed in behind her, drawing her to my chest. She clutched my arm that settled between her breasts and drew it upward so my palm opened and covered her heart. It raced even in her sleep, and I worried she was still frightened of me. Then I thought of her face when she shaved my jaw and cut my hair. Her pupils dilated. She was attracted to me.

I was leaving no doubt that I was attracted to her, and it wasn't because she was the only female on the island. I couldn't keep my hands from her, and I thought back to that night. I wanted to take her, but something stopped me. The look in her eyes. That moment we shared, I couldn't follow through with what Rick wanted to do.

*"We're going to play this my way,"* I had said as I slipped down my pants, enough to release me. I stood at her entrance, taking willpower I never knew I had to withstand entering her.

*"I'm going to move, blink if you understand."* Her eyes closed and she turned her head, but I needed her to see it wasn't me that planned to harm her. The damage had already been done, and I wanted to kill Rick. If she became one of his charges, I would instantly request her.

*I rocked my hips, the hard length of me caressing her inner thigh. The pleasure was unbearable. The heat of her skin rubbed against mine. I licked two fingers and pressed them over sensitive folds. My eyes closed, and I shuddered, fighting the control. I wanted inside her, but then I looked at her eyes again. I slipped a leg over hers, hoping to disguise from the others that I hadn't entered her. I wanted it to look real. My mouth lowered to hers again and I spoke against her gagged lips She didn't seem to hear me, and I worried she was drugged. The camera was recording. Rick was encouraging, but I couldn't perform. Never in my life had I had to fake an orgasm. It was harder than I thought, as I rolled on a condom and pretended to release inside the latex.*

*My false finish was interrupted with a shout from that weaseling bartender.*

*"Get off her. She's not one of them." Rick went for the kid instantly, and I thought he'd lay him in the ground. Instead, he hollered for Rory to take care of him. As Rory had been the camera man, the show was over, and she was free. But she was dead in her eyes, dry of tears, and staring blankly up at the ceiling. I hated myself in that moment, and I reached to help her. When she turned away from me, my anger flared.*

*"Suit yourself," I snapped, adjusting my pants and leaving her behind.*

I tugged her tighter to me, burying my nose in the nape of her neck. I'd already apologized, but a million *I'm sorry's* would never be enough. She was still unsure of me, slightly frightened. The fidgeting in her sleep proved it, but I vowed to all things above, that I'd never let her hurt again.

+ +

"Tack." The sound of my name loudly rushed through my ears. A palm pressed against my face, forcing me backward. I woke with a start, finding her under me, breathing heavily. I was groping her. My hand massaged over one breast as my hips bucked forward, finding friction in the heat of her core.

"Shit," I hissed, abruptly scrambling off her, realizing I'd been fucking her in my dream, completing the act that I started but hadn't finished.

I lay on my back, my dick throbbing, my heart racing as I stared at the dark ceiling. My thoughts collided with sorrow and my need to be inside her. For a moment, I thought she'd seen my dream, recalled my memory, and realized my desire. How could she not know how I felt after what I'd been doing? I wanted nothing to break this spell we had started, but I was ruining everything.

She sat up and flipped her legs to the side of the mattress. I wrapped my arm around her waist and tugged her back.

"Don't go," I breathed. "I'm sorry."

To my surprise, she spun to face me. Burying her head in my chest so I couldn't see her in the darkness. I couldn't make out her expression or read her body language, other than feel her body quivering against mine.

"What is it, baby?" I asked, but knowing the answer. I'd scared her again. My fingers skimmed over her body, reaching for her chin. Tipping her head upright, I still had no way to focus on her eyes in the dim light.

"I need to go back to my house," she whispered, her breath shaky.

"It's the middle of the night. It's too dark. Go back to sleep. I've got you," I said, wrapping my arms around her and holding her tighter against me, but knowing I was the nightmare who caused her to shake. Her lips hovered over my skin, the warmth of her breath tickling my chest. I wanted her to kiss me—give me a sign she accepted my apology. Softly, her lips met my flesh where she lingered over my heart.

The connection was like a jolt of electricity, and I felt something I'd never felt before. My body stiffened—petrified, in fact. I was terrified of the sensation coursing through my veins. Her lips at my heart were a live wire, reviving me over and over again. She shook her head as she released me, and her hair brushed at my damp skin. The tent was warm with two bodies so close together, but I'd do anything she asked to be warmer, to get closer. She was in control, but I was at the edge of mine.

Her hips rolled forward, brushing her core dangerously close to the heavy weight of my stiff dick. It had to be an accident. On the verge of denotation, I groaned. I wanted her too much, too fast. My fingers folded into the sheer material of her skirt, clutching at her dress.

*I can't do this*, I thought. I was on the verge of taking as a way to prove I needed her, but I wanted her to willingly give herself to me. I wanted her permission, but I didn't have it yet. She didn't trust me, and I sensed it with the stiffness of her movement, the ragged inhale of her breaths, and the moisture leaking onto my chest. She was crying, and I was to fault for the salty liquid streaking her face. My breath hitched.

"I can't do this." The words were harshly stated as if more to myself than to her. It wasn't rejection. I was saving her from me. She rolled to her back, and I followed her, reaching for her face, swiping at the tears moistening her cheeks. Her hand came forward and pressed against my wrist.

"Get off me," she whispered. My chest pinched with her misunderstanding.

"Mouse, I didn't mean—" The motion of her sitting up cut me off.

"Get off me!" she yelled, and I scrambled back from the bed, swiping a hand through my hair as I stepped to the front of the tent. I couldn't look back. I wouldn't be able to see her face. I wouldn't be able to *look* her in the face. After all that I'd done, she'd never forgive me, and I had to accept these facts.

# 21

## The Island Hears Your Sorrow

Like the tiny mouse he called her, she scrambled from the tent and scampered through the jungle forest. Her thoughts were a jumble of recollection. She'd reached for his hand during the night and covered her heart, hoping he could feel the racing within—the fear and excitement—that rippled through her veins, tickling the fine hairs of her body with hope. No one had ever spoken to her in that way before.

*It's dark without you.*

The words slithered through her as she trekked through the dawning day, still dark within the heavy bush of the island. He hadn't meant what he said, she decided. He couldn't know how empty the darkness was for her. How lonely she felt, longing for someone.

*I'd love someone to care for me.* A sob escaped as she traveled stealthily through the greenery, climbing higher, away from the beach, away from his tent, hoping to lose herself in the island. She admitted one of her darkest secrets to someone who could use it against her. And he rejected her.

He did not care about her. He cared about nothing. If he couldn't take her by force, like one of his businesses to be bought and broken, he wasn't interested. She could give herself willingly, but that wasn't how he wanted it. He held her back against his warm chest, but he wanted to take her, even in his sleep.

Another sob escaped, and she covered her mouth, though there was no one to hear her cries. He had been a dream. *He wasn't real*, she told herself. His sorrow. His repentance. It was a lie.

He'd shown he could be caring when she was sick, sharing with his steak feast, but he could not care *about* her. She shook her head. He wanted to control someone.

*I can't do this.* His words ripped a chasm through her chest, her heart pierced with pain. She tripped and fell among the thick roots and twisted limbs at her feet. Pressing upward, she continued to scamper through the brush, seeing light up ahead. Bursting through the thickness of greenery, she came to a small, open clearing and fell to her knees, feeling the warmth of the sun on her clammy skin. She lay flat on the surface of rich earth, letting the heat of the dirt press against her cheeks, damp from the tears she hadn't notice falling. She hadn't given them tears before, but now they fell. Her heart raced, pressed against the island floor, and she willed herself to become one with her surroundings.

*Take the power from him*, she heard whispered in her head. Closing her eyes, she felt the beat of her heart, the pulse of the island under her cheeks, and the sound of the breeze overhead. She imagined him at her back, enveloping her in love, not control, and she wrapped her hand over his as she had last night. She slid it downward, covering her breast, feeling the sad beat under her skin.

"Juliet," she heard whispered in the wind, but she kept her eyes closed. She had no words to speak. She only wanted to imagine she could dominate him. She wanted to speak through touch—controlling his over hers. She pretended it was his fingers squeezing, ripening her nipple to a sharp peak. A steady beat increased between her thighs, and she took slow breaths to match the tempo. Her teeth bit back a moan threatening to escape. She arched her back, recalling the connection of his excitement pressed along the seam of her backside. In her head, she lowered his hand, letting the heat of his palm cover her belly. She used her free fingers to pull up her dress, guiding his hands under the material. She wore bikini panties under her dress. How stupid she'd been. To think she'd risked herself again, and with *him*, of all men.

She pressed two fingers between needy folds, increasing the achy pulse. She imagined his fingers moving in a circular motion, a pattern of friction, similar to the slow tap of a drum.

The breeze picked up, caressing her neck. *Like touching you, Mouse*, she heard him murmur against her skin. His fingers took control, but her hand covered his. The sensation was so real. The pressure so intense. He could please a woman. She wanted him to please her.

*Show me how*, the wind whispered. The words mixed with the breeze, brushing back the hair at her sweaty temples. Her tears had subsided for the moment. Her concentration was on the physical connection she shared with this man. The mere thought of his fingers between her thighs heightened her pleasure. An exhale of air escaped her lips as her body moved in a dancing rhythm. The beat of island drums rang in her head, matching the pulse at her core. Her hips followed the thumping, vibrating over fingers nimble and greedy. Her body became an instrument. Suddenly, wild with need, she clamped down on the back of his imaginary hand at her core and thrust a finger inside, feeling the length of his digit filling her. She'd climbed to her knees, panting in need, clutching her thighs together. A second finger forced its way inside and she let out a grunt as her free hand dug into the hard, packed dirt at her tips.

Her body became something other than her own. She was an island goddess, paying homage to herself, using him as her fantasy. She would not allow him to stop the rhythm, the touch, demanding it until she reached her peak. His imaginary fingers danced inside her, a sliding movement creating its own music. Her fist pounded the earth as she screamed to release. An animalistic roar rolled from her throat, and she called out his name. She refused to be his mouse. She did not want to be tamed by him.

Her name whispered in the air like a lullaby, lilting around her ears. It didn't match the slowing tempo between her thighs, but the sound sent a wave of anger through her.

"Just one," she yelled aloud, repeatedly his words. Just once, she wanted a man to care about her, and she hoped her voice carried down the slope of the island, directly to him. *Hear me*, she whispered in her mind.

*Just once,* she thought again as she felt wetness slick down her inner thighs and sweat curl down her hairline. Tears filled her eyes again, and she lowered herself to the ground in exhaustion, like a mouse hidden in the field. *No*, she told herself. She was a lioness, and she would rule over him. But as the pulse within her lessened, and her heart rate lowered to a normal beat, she felt the calm rhythm of the island under her tear-stained cheeks. Her lips sought the dirt like they reached for his chest, and she knew it was too late.

She cared about him, and that meant he ruled over her.

# 22

# Day 41 – Juliet

Seven full days I'd gone without a visit from him. I didn't hear his voice or seek him out. *It wasn't healthy focusing on him*, I told myself. I'd already followed him once, and that had been the mistake of a lifetime. It was all because of him that I entered that room.

I remained holed up in the tree house or took long treks through the jungle as I had a week before. My discoveries led me in circles, winding and weaving through areas that one moment looked similar and another seemed diverse. It never mattered. I was on a small island without much land mass. One inch appeared the same as the next except for the white beach near where his tent stood and the small enclosed cove with Lillian's dock. I wandered letting the exercise distract my thoughts.

In a moment of weakness, after my self-soothing toss in the dirt, I allowed myself to remember him from that night. I'd been asked to wait on a room on the third floor, and I took the assignment out of curiosity, but also because of him. I didn't know much about him, but I marveled at the cut of his jaw, the gleam of his eyes, and the crooked smile on his lips. I was attracted to him beyond anything I'd felt before but recognized the giddiness of infatuation with a man out of my league. Still, I went when asked. I'd been told it was a special request.

The moment I entered the room, I sensed the tension. The subtle glances in my direction. The appraisal of my body in the skimpy uniform—little black, skin-tight dress. The air was charged with a nervous energy, and I looked up at him, his eyes glassy with drink. I thought he saw me, but he looked through me. Distracted, that's when I was captured.

*"Cooperate, and your promotion will bring you wealth."*

I had wanted a raise, but not like this. I struggled without results as I was quickly bound at the wrists and gagged after I screamed. I couldn't imagine the other men would stand around and watch, but as I noticed their movement, as if in slow motion or a dream, jackets removed, and shirt sleeves rolled up, it was if the men prepared to relax and watch a performance. My body jackknifed, and I was thrown on the leather couch. Roughly, my dress was removed, and I lay exposed in my demi-bra and thong.

There I stopped. I didn't need to remember the rest.

*Look at me,* I had willed with my eyes, keeping my concentration on Tack while I was taken by Rick. He paid no attention to me. My guard had been down for only a moment, my distraction was him, and a sharp slap to my face was the result. A mouse trapped by the lure of the cat, they had caught me.

*Never again,* I told myself, walking with my head higher as I explored the jungle around me. And yet, his body rutting over mine had released a nervous energy, one I couldn't deny on that morning as he offered his apology and then rejected me. My toss in the dirt had been a baptism, freeing me sexually, liberating my voice as I screamed, drying my tears as I cried. I would take and not be taken again.

+ +

The call of my name was a whisper, but it caught my attention as I sat in my chair at the square table. I'd been working on writing my self-reflective discoveries every moment I wasn't sleeping or walking. My body had toned with the extensive exercise, and my eating improved. I didn't anticipate Lillian and Franco for four days, and the rugged voice wasn't either of theirs. I paused in my writing, listening intently.

"I'm dreaming him again," I said aloud, telling myself it was only the wind.

"Juliet," I heard louder, distinctly present beneath my tree house. I lowered my head to the desk, rolling it back and forth on the notebook.

"I have to stop doing this," I muttered into the pages.

"Let me up, Juliet, or I'm coming in without your permission," he snapped. My head shot up, and I realized he could have entered anytime he wanted, but he hadn't. He'd only been uninvited once and that was when he saved me from the snake. I walked to the latch for the ladder, my legs heavy with dread. Kicking at the rope structure, it slipped through the hole in the platform and tumbled to his reach. I stepped back as he climbed, my heart racing with each creak of the rope, straining with the weight of him. As his head crested the opening, I turned for my room. I didn't think my heart could stand the first look of him, so ready to burst with anticipation and trepidation.

I sat in my chair at the table, trying to appear casual while my body quaked. I fisted my hands in the hem of my shorts. Sweat instantly slicked my palms.

He passed through the doorway, swiping back the jagged cut of his hair, grown out slightly in a week. His jaw was covered in light stubble, and my breath caught at the appearance of him. His eyes gleamed brighter than I'd ever seen, matching the leaves outside my tree house window. He was breathtaking, and I hated him at the same time my chest clenched with relief at seeing him.

He scanned the room, taking in the layers of books and open notebooks across the table. There were two chairs set on either side of the table where I sat but he selected the trunk at the end of the bed. His long legs bent and he balanced his elbows on his thighs. I remained silent, willing him to speak first.

"You left," he whispered.

"You didn't really want me to stay," I offered, my voice harsher than I expected. He instantly looked up.

"I want so many things, Juliet. Some of them I can't even articulate because I don't have a name for them." His comment startled me and I blinked.

"I—"

"I have things I want to say." His tone was sharp, and I was taken aback again. I shifted in my seat, sliding my sweaty palms down the sides of my shorts and then nervously curling loose hairs behind my ear. He watched the movement, following the stroke of my fingers before swallowing and beginning.

"Rick Fontaine was my best friend—"

"I don't want to hear this," I cut him off, looking away from him, Rick's name on his lips was a sharp sting to my cheeks, the bite of a snake, and I trembled. My jaw clenched. I was letting this go. Him go. Them go. I didn't want to think about that night again.

"You're going to hear me out, and then you can kick me out. But I'm speaking first." His voice remained short.

*We're going to play this my way* trickled through my head, but I could only blink in response, the reply he wanted from me.

"Rick Fontaine was my best friend, and he was an asshole. He should have been killed twenty times over by drug dealers and disgruntled women, but I loved him, in a strange way because he was my friend. I didn't agree with all of his practices. It was always a competition between us—never set by me, but by him. It was just the way we were. He worked for what he had, while I had it handed to me. He didn't openly begrudge me, but it was apparent with every risk, every dare, every suggestion for trouble, that he envied me and how easily things happened for me."

He paused and I stared at him, sweat trickling down my neck. The idea of sympathy for Rick Fontaine made my stomach toss, and the pressure of vomit rose inside me. I swallowed the bile-taste in my mouth.

"He had taken on a lifestyle that suited his need to be in control. He wanted to prove he was better than others, and his club was one way to do this. The Front Door was going to be an investment for me. He needed money, but he'd never take a gift, and I was intrigued, as I am too often with anything that would piss off my father. To prove myself, Rick suggested this initiation, but he wanted first dibs."

"First dibs," I mouthed.

"It was so fucked up. We would each get a turn. Rick, myself, Rory and Smack."

"I was there," I bit, reminding him that I was in the room, and his recall was coming at my expense.

"Something happened to me. I couldn't do it, but I didn't know how to back out. The look in your eyes." He paused. "I thought if I could just get through it, get it over with..." His voice faltered, and he combed through his hair, sitting upright.

"It was wrong. On so many levels it was wrong. It had nothing to do with you directly, and everything to do with Rick."

"It was all me," I choked. "Why me? Why any woman?" The sickness in me grew, and nausea crept up my throat.

"It had to be you, according to Rick, but I don't know why."

"I wouldn't have him. He made advances and crude suggestions, but I refused him. I'd had years of practice avoiding my uncle, so Rick was easy to push away."

Tack shook his head. "But you can't push a guy like Rick, so ready to prove himself, prove he has control of a situation."

"Isn't that what you want? Control? Domination? Tear down, rip apart." My hands twisted and turned for emphasis, shaking with the need to punch something, and my intention focused on him. I wanted to slap him. I wanted to hate him. I wanted to take back what he took from me.

"I thought I did, I just..." He stared off toward the tree trunk centering the room. "There was this moment when I looked at you under me, and I just...I wanted you to give yourself instead of me taking."

If he had cut himself and spilled blood on my floor, I don't think he could have looked anymore raw and vulnerable than he did in that moment. But I had no sympathy for him.

"I have nightmares. I couldn't sleep for weeks. When I went to get my final paycheck, Brandon assured me Rick wasn't present. I should have had it mailed to me, but I didn't have an address to send it to. I'd left Chellie's apartment. I slept at the university a few nights in an empty dorm. Killing Rick brought me no satisfaction. It only started a new set of nightmares. I'll never forgive myself, and I might never forgive you." The words were venom spewing from my mouth, but they were things I'd longed to say. He had to know my feelings were strong. I hated myself, but I hated him as well.

"I'm sorry," he muttered, lowering his head.

"Weak," I whispered. His head shot up again. "You think I'm weak, that's why you wanted to take me. It had nothing to do with me, but more about you and your weakness. You need control to make you feel important. To make you feel worthy. You take because you have no understanding of giving. Asking would be a weakness." My chest rose and fell with each statement, the adrenaline coursing through my body in such a surge I nearly choked on it.

His shoulders slumped forward, and he rested his elbows on his thighs again. His hands clasped together, the knuckles whitening with the pressure. I don't know if the words struck a chord, or if he wanted to act on his anger.

"I might never be able to love a man because of you," I snapped. "I might never trust one again. I want things." I beat on my chest with my fist as I stood. "And you've taken them from me with your little game. I want to believe it can be more than it was with Rick and *you*. I think it can, but I can't get past the pain in here." I poked at my own chest, signaling my heart. "Even when I ache here." I slid my finger between my breasts down to the edge of my zipper.

His eyes opened wide and he stood as well. With two large steps, he crossed the room, his green eyes bright as he focused on my finger. Standing before me, he shocked me further by folding to his knees. His fingers came to my hips.

"Tell me how to make it better for you, and I will."

I didn't answer him. My hand slipped away from the front of my shorts. My fingers twitched to run through his hair as they had after the cut a week ago, but my heart raced and my thoughts conflicted. His hands released my hips, and he sat back on his ankles. His palms came to rest on his knees, his eyes lowering to them.

"I'll be your submissive. Control me. Tell me what you need physically, emotionally, and I'll give you anything." He peeked up at me. "Anything."

My hands could no longer hold back, and I reached for his hair. Combing through the soft locks, my brows pinched. I didn't understand. I didn't know what he was offering, or how I was to respond. His forehead came forward to rest on my lower belly. Two thick hands gripped my hips, and he tugged gently at the pockets of my shorts.

"Anything you ask," he offered on his knees. "Just don't leave me again."

# 23

# Days 41 – 44 - Tack

For four days, we learned about one another. We didn't see each other naked. We didn't touch. I marveled at how we seemed to have worked in reverse. We fucked, we foreplayed, we kissed, we snuggled…and now, we nothing-ed. But we were learning about one another, and some of the conversations were difficult. She told me about her uncle and some of his intentions toward her. I told her about my mother and her pills. She told me about the accident during a storm that killed her parents. I told her more about my father's manipulation. We did not speak of Rick again, nor of that night. We focused on one another's history instead.

Most of our conversations took place as we walked. We traveled the island, seeking places we hadn't seen, and trying to memorize the land. It was a beautiful, tropical haven if only each moment didn't still feel like a punishment.

"Garvey is coming tomorrow. I don't have a set time for his arrival. They just arrive when they want, but I want to see you afterward," I said.

"Lillian will be coming as well. Maybe it's best to take a day off," she suggested. I reached for her hand and tugged her to stop. She spun as she was walking before me.

"I don't want a day off. Each day, I feel as if I'm in a dream, and when night falls, I'm afraid to sleep and end the dream." The words were raw, the emotion behind them displaying my vulnerability. I didn't want her to disappear again. A man on the verge of insanity was the only way to explain those days she'd been missing. I hadn't found her in her tree house, or if she was present, she ignored me. I never stumbled upon her in the pond or even walking through the trees. It had been lonely without her.

On this island, I'd discovered what was truly my greatest fear—I didn't like to be alone. While I thought the banishment would be an excellent respite from the pressure of my father and the weight of my past, being alone was a trigger for me. I couldn't handle myself. Guilt haunted me when I thought of what we'd done to this beautiful girl sharing herself with me in solidarity of our circumstances. But it was deeper than that. Being alone made me face the fact I was alone. My father wanted what he wanted of me. My friends were the same. It was a game to conform to others' wishes, and I was losing when I had to face myself. I did the things I did so as not to be lonely. I wanted the attention—negative and wrong—so I didn't have to face my greatest fear—being alone because someone wouldn't want me for me.

She smiled slowly, though the light didn't reach her eyes. The smile she was growing confident to give me had been diminished with my late-night sleep-rutting. It was trying my patience to win it back, but my patience had surprisingly grown. If we spent enough time together, I felt confident I would see it again. Some day. Hopefully soon.

"Fine, I'll come find you near evening."

"No, let me come to you," I said. "I don't want you wandering in the dark."

She tugged her hand from mine and crossed her arms. Her hip hitched and she scowled. She actually looked beautiful while her lip pouted.

"I've wandered a few times through the darkness," she said, staking her claim in knowing the path to and from my door.

"Yes, you have, and it wasn't really safe," I replied, curling a piece of loose hair behind her ear. She didn't flinch at my touch, and I took this as a good sign. I didn't wish to test her any further, though, so I dropped my hand.

"Fine," she muttered.

"Fine," I teased.

++

"Have you danced?" Garvey asked. He sat on the same stump with a knife in his hand, whittling at a strip of wood. Colton sat in the sand next to his father. My leg jiggled as I sat across from them.

"No, I haven't danced," I scoffed. I wasn't fucking dancing.

"Have you not learned anything?" Garvey asked, still concentrating on the stick in his hand.

"I've learned plenty of things," I snapped.

"I see your anger is still intact," Colton offered sarcastically. My eyes shifted over his head, ignoring him, and gazing at the trees that lead to Juliet.

"It is," Garvey said, and I noticed his eyes followed mine. Turning back to me, he added, "But you do seem calmer. A little."

"I am," I said, but my leg continued to bounce up and down. I visibly clamped a hand at my thigh to stop the motion.

"You need to dance. Let out the energy."

I sighed. "Let me ask again, what is the point in dancing?"

"Dance is an expression of emotion. You must pick an animal, one you've encountered on the island. Think about it. What can you learn from it? Dance the motions of the animal. Reflect."

I shook my head. "I'll think about it."

"You'll do it," Garvey commanded, but his voice remained monotone. My eyes drifted back in the direction of Juliet's tree house.

"You seem distracted," Garvey said, interrupting my gaze and I noticed again his eyes were focused in the same area as mine. "Are you okay?"

"I'm fine," I snapped.

"Maybe we should stay the night with you?"

"No!" The harshness of my tone startled even me and I swiped a hand through my hair. "I mean, no, I'm doing okay. You don't need to stay." I didn't want them hanging out and ruining a chance to see Juliet.

"I see," Garvey said, looking over his shoulder one last time before turning back to me. His face remained stoic, but the dark orbs of his eyes danced. If I didn't know better, I'd say he was laughing at me.

"Your hair looks different," Colton observed, narrowing his eyes on my hand that continued to work through the smooth locks.

"Yeah, I figured out a few things so I could cut it better."

Colton's eyes remained pinched, staring at me like he could read my secrets. They didn't ask about the girl this time, and I no longer wished to share her presence. The thought seemed to trigger Colton to speak.

"Still seeing that girl?" The wording caught me off guard. He asked so casually it was as if he wondered if I was dating Juliet. Reminding myself he didn't believe she was on the island, I chose my answer carefully.

"I don't care if you believe she's here. I don't need to prove anything to you. I only need to prove things to myself."

The silence was sharp as Garvey stopped whittling. Looking up at him, his eyes were focused on mine, brows raised in surprise. He pursed his lips and slowly nodded.

"Well, you are actually learning something."

I wanted to wipe the smirk off his face because I didn't know what he meant, but I let it slide. I didn't have time for a confrontation with them. I wanted them off my island.

"We brought more books," Garvey said, pointing with the stick toward a sack. I'd taken to long hours of reading with no television, no stock reports, no merger stats to review. I'd re-read a handful of classics, intermingled with some informational texts. I stood to search the pile.

"*Robinson Crusoe*?" I questioned as I held the book in the air. "*The Lord of the Flies*? Really?"

"It was my turn to pick," Colton offered, pleased with his selection. One book was about a man shipwrecked on an island, and the second was about a group of boys' whose plane wrecked and they worked survival of the fittest to the extreme by killing one of their own.

"*The Little Prince*?" I stared at the thin book in my hand. *A child's story*, I instantly thought. "Interesting choice."

"You might learn something from it as well," Garvey suggested. I thumbed through the pages and slipped it into my back pocket. "Do the dance," he added, patting my shoulder before leaving me again.

++

After dinner, she sat at her table working on her papers, and I lay on her bed to read. I brought *The Little Prince* by Antoine de Saint-Exupéry with me, sensing a kinship with this young man who wandered the universe, asking questions and discovering things.

"I don't think you are my rose," I said, breaking the comfortable silence we had developed around one another. She looked up from her notes and shifted to face me. "I haven't nurtured you enough. You aren't under a glass with me. I think you are the fox."

"Instead of a mouse?" she giggled. I'd developed a soft spot for that sound over the last few days. It was a rare gift, and I cherished each time she directed it at me.

"You are still a mouse, but maybe more of a vixen," I said, wiggling my eyebrows over the edge of the book.

"How so?" she chuckled again, standing and approaching the bed. I scooted over, hoping she would take the hint and lay down next to me.

"You tempt me." She stopped at the side of the small mattress.

"But I am not sly or sneaky like a vixen," she replied, her voice rising in a playful octave.

"True." I paused to tap the book on my chin. "But I am smitten by you."

The comment stopped us both, and our eyes met. She didn't blink. The air in the room held its breath.

"I mean, I am taken by you." My voice lowered, and I shifted my eyes to the words on the page but was unable to focus on any of them.

"Read the passage to me," she said, sitting on the bed, and I tapped the book on the pillow, signaling she should join me by lying down.

*"Who are you?" asked the little prince, and added, "You are very pretty to look at."* I looked over at her after I read, and stared at her a moment. She was beautiful lying next to me, and my heart skipped a beat.

*"I am a fox," the fox said*, she read, breaking my gaze. She nudged my arm, encouraging me to read my part.

*"Come and play with me," proposed the little prince. "I am so unhappy."* I stopped at the words. How true it was, or had been, before coming to this island. I wasn't happy, but I didn't have time to dwell as Juliet spoke her part.

*"I cannot play with you,"* the fox said. *"I am not tamed."* Juliet shifted her voice while she read, so I lowered mine as I continued.

*"Ah! Please excuse me,"* said the little prince.

*But, after some thought, he added:*

*"What does that mean--'tame'?"* I read.

*"You do not live here,"* said the fox. *"What is it that you are looking for?"* How true the words seemed, and I considered the question spoken in Juliet's voice.

*"I am looking for men,"* said the little prince. *"What does that mean--'tame'?"* I read again.

*"Men,"* said the fox. *"They have guns, and they hunt. It is very disturbing. They also raise chickens. These are their only interests. Are you looking for chickens?"*

"Chickens?" I interjected.

"Keep reading." She nudged my arm again with her shoulder which pressed against my skin. She'd shifted to her side and was focused on the book in my hands.

*"No,"* said the little prince. *"I am looking for friends. What does that mean--'tame'?"* I stared at the words. I once considered Rick a friend, but he hadn't really been.

*"It is an act too often neglected,"* said the fox. *"It means to establish ties."*

*"'To establish ties'?"* I swallowed hard after I read this line. I had no ties to anyone. I drifted.

*"Just that,"* said the fox. *"To me, you are still nothing more than a little boy who is just like a hundred thousand other little boys. And I have no need of you. And you, on your part, have no need of me. To you, I am nothing more than a fox, like a hundred thousand other foxes. But if you tame me, then we shall need each other. To me, you will be unique in all the world. To you, I shall be unique in all the world..."*

"I think I'd like to be the fox, actually," she said.

"You want to be tamed?" The idea of dominating her returned and tension filled the air, yet somehow taming meant more than domination. It seemed to mean responsibility, caring for something. I'd already promised she could dominate me, instead, but I was changing my mind.

"I want to be friends," she whispered, her breath brushed my skin, and the heat between us rose again.

"Am I one to you? I'm certainly no prince," I said, my voice lowering. I wanted to be her friend. I wanted to be so much more.

"You are a thousand little boys until you learn to tame me, to be invested in me, as I am invested in you. Then you will be my friend like the fox says," she added. Her violet eyes were playful, sparkling in a way I'd never seen before. Gone was the hatred. Gone was the desire. Gone was fear. In its place was something more, and it pleased me.

I groaned. "I still say you are a vixen."

# 24

# Day 47 - Juliet

The heat of the day was oppressing, but the nights refreshing with the ocean breeze. We sat on the edge of the water in the dimming daylight, staring silently out at the calm water. Midnight blue was catching the waves as blackness chased it. There was no sunset tonight, only clouds on the horizon.

"I made this for you." Presenting him with the braided bracelet I'd made with leaves rolled into string, I held my breath. I'd never given a man a gift, let alone something I'd made.

"Aw, did you make me a friendship bracelet?" he teased, and I pushed at his shoulder. I bit my lip, suddenly self-conscious. It seemed foolish after all.

He took it from me, spinning it over and over with his fingers. His tips traveled the thick circle, and he appeared to be admiring my handiwork, but I braced myself for another tease. He extended his wrist, one I imagined typically held an expensive watch, and he slipped the band over his hand. He twisted his wrist back and forth.

"Why did you make this for me?" he asked, his voice lacking the teasing tone I expected. I shrugged.

"I wanted to thank you for saving my life, twice." His eyes were intense, and I looked away, cursing myself for the offering. It was a silly idea, I decided.

"Mouse," he whispered, tracing a finger down my cheek to my jaw, and gently forcing me to look at him. "It was my pleasure to save you. And thank you. This is really special. No one's ever given me something like this before."

"A leaf bracelet," I joked, trying to lessen the sudden seriousness around him.

"A handmade gift. It means you really thought about this and then took the time to make it specifically for me. It fits perfectly. I'll always wear it. Thank you." I prepared to make another joke about his wearing it forever, but the earnestness in his voice stopped me. His appreciation was heartfelt, and a soft kiss on my cheek surprised me.

Suddenly, the sky crackled and lightning raced upward. I flinched in surprise.

Tack's arm came around my shoulders. He rubbed up and down and then released me. Strangely, I longed for him to continue holding me, but the touches had been few and far between since our friendship started. A brush here. A hair tuck there. A finger sliding down my jaw, but nothing deeper. I'd fallen asleep next to him the night he read *The Little Prince*. After our interchange of reading about the fox, I let him continue, drifting off with the inflection of his rugged, but gentle voice. To both our surprise, he slept as well, and we woke with my hands wrapped around his arm like I was holding onto him for dear life. I hadn't been dreaming, or at least I couldn't remember if I had, but I'd somehow latched onto him during the night. He didn't say anything about it. His smile brightened, and he whispered "Good Morning" before brushing my forehead with his lips and rolling off the bed.

The lightning flashed again and thunder echoed in the distance. I flinched a second time.

"Don't like lightning?" he asked, and I squinted out at the dark sea.

"I was home alone. There was a bad storm, and I remember waking at a certain point in the night, hearing the sharp crack of thunder. It was 2:43 a.m. I hadn't been able to go back to sleep, and I lay there breathing heavily, willing the lightning to go away. I hadn't known they died yet, at that exact time, but ever since that night, I just can't shake the fear that lightning means bad things." I scooped my hands through the cool, white sand, as my voice drifted.

"I won't let it hurt you," he said, and I smiled weakly at the comment. "I'd save you again and again if needed." He owed me. It hesitated in the space after what he said. He felt responsible for what happened—he owed me, to save me if anything ever happened again. I sighed in frustration. He'd been saying things more often like this. Little compliments or startling words said casually, and on the surface, they seemed sweet, but underneath seemed imbued with a deeper meaning. My heart foolishly skipped a beat with each one shared, hopeful that it might mean more to him, knowing it only meant something to me.

The sea wasn't curling and cursing near us, but it looked like a storm was definitely over the ocean.

"I wish we had a boat," he said, and I twisted to look at him.

"Why?"

"I'd like to go sailing out there."

"On a night like this?" I choked.

"No, Mouse, during the day. It would be cool to skip across the water, especially when it's so calm." He held up his hands, palms down, and spread them apart as if imitating the ocean. "I'd like to take you sailing."

"Why don't you ask Garvey for one?" I snorted softly. "You have the whole country club thing going here anyway." She twisted to glance over her shoulder, admiring my extravagant beachside tent with camp furniture and the hammock in the trees.

"You're the one with a real bed," Tack teased. "But honestly, I don't think they'd give me a boat. They'd be afraid I'd try to escape." He leaned back on his hands and let his toes slide in the sand.

"Would you?" I asked. He let his chin fall to his shoulder as he looked at me.

"Not anymore."

My lips curled slowly in response. My mouth moistened with need. I wanted to taste him again, when we were like this, when he was sweet.

"Why don't you build one?"

He laughed with a puff of air. "How?"

"Well, I don't know," I said. "You're the ship builder's son. Don't you know how to build one?"

He stared at me a long moment before turning his eyes back to the ocean.

"Huh," he huffed.

"What?"

"You're right." For some reason, we let those words linger between us before he walked me back to my tree house.

++

"I found it," he shouted the next day when I came to his camp. His voice trilled with excitement.

"Found what?" I laughed, joining in his enthusiasm before I even knew what brought it on. I liked when he laughed. His face brightened and he looked less edgy, younger even.

"The perfect tree. I bet we could scoop it out somehow and attach some smaller limbs to work as double outriggers."

"Like a canoe?" I laughed again.

"Sort of, but with outriggers for balance, like they use in the Philippines."

"Have you been to the Philippines?" I intended to laugh, but then I remembered his background. He'd probably been to every corner of the world when I was just happy to escape a trailer park in Alabama.

"I have." I shook my head in response.

"Come on, Mouse," he said, holding out his hand, and I couldn't deny him with the eagerness of his voice.

For a week, we worked on gutting the large log he found from a downed tree. He was patient as he explained what he needed me to do to help build the long, strap-like arches that stretched over the canoe-shaped boat for balance.

"I don't know if this will hold both of us," I said skeptically, as we grew closer to our finished product.

"Well, it just has to, because I'm not testing it without you, first mate," he teased. He was playful, like a child, like a thousand little princes, I thought, and I warmed to him more at his enjoyment in building something from scratch. For a man who said he thrived on tearing things apart, his hands were equally diligent at putting something together.

"We won't go far," he promised, looking up to see me staring at him. "I won't let anything happen to you," he promised once again. He must have questioned something in my expression. I was beginning to think it was ominous as if something bad were coming, and he kept wanting to assure me he'd protect me. I shook off the thought and continued with my twisting and tying of long grasses and stripped leaves that we were using as rope to secure the outrigging.

On day fifty-six, we took our maiden voyage.

"We'll go just to the edge of the bay and back," he promised, but I worried a riptide was out there. If we fell overboard, we couldn't swim back.

"I think mice prefer to stay on dry land," I said, teasing him, but he held up his hand, offering it for me to take. He led me to one side of the craft.

"We'll have to work together to get it out there, but I'll let you hop in before it's too deep. We each have an oar, and I'll tell you how to stroke once we are settled." He winked at me. "*The Vixen* awaits."

"*The Vixen*?" I questioned.

"Every boat needs a name, and every boat is a *she*, so this one is *The Vixen*, named after one of our building crew." He winked at me again, and I blushed.

"Foxes like dry land as well," I teased.

"Yes, but a vixen is sly and cunning, and can handle any situation dealt to her. She knows when to trust in her captain, as well."

I shook my head again. He made no sense, but he crossed behind the boat we'd designed together and walked the double outrigger out to sea. When we were calf-deep, he told me to jump in. I fumbled a bit, not finding leverage with the water, but he held the boat steady enough and patiently waited for me. Once inside, we both sighed a breath of relief. She wasn't sinking.

He jumped in after a few more steps, and I screamed when the craft elevated on my end with the sudden weight on the back. I held my breath, preparing to capsize when my portion of the boat returned to the water. Slowly, we skimmed across the ocean bay.

"She's sailing," I yelled behind me.

"She's perfect," he chanted back. I twisted in my seat to find a brilliant smile on his face, white teeth fully on display. He paddled like he'd done this every day, stroking side to side to keep us moving straight ahead. Without his shirt, and in his tan skin, he looked like a voyager set to see the world. He looked happy.

# 25

# Day 60 – Tack

I almost dreaded Garvey's visit, but he brought fresh supplies and occasionally new linens. I hadn't mastered washing sheets that well. He never brought letters. I wasn't allowed communication with the outside world, but I had to ask.

"Has anyone asked about me? Has my dad?"

Garvey looked up from admiring my small boat. I was proud of my first attempt at building something. I'd had some trial and error in the design but it felt amazing to build something. I hadn't worked on anything like that since my grandfather had me help him sand an old wooden boat in the back dry dock. The thought was so ancient in my memory, it was hazy, but I saw the outline of my grandfather, working slowly as he pushed the sanding block along the grain of the wood.

*"You treat her right, stroke her like she needs, and she'll skim like a dolphin through the sea. You're a lucky sailor then,"* he whispered in my recollection. His reverence spoke of the boat, but now as a man myself, I sensed he was trying to impart some deeper wisdom on me.

"You know I can't tell you anything," Garvey said softly, letting his hand coast over the curve of the canoe. "You built this yourself?" he asked.

Irritated that he couldn't even hint about my parents, I snapped in response. "Nah, my monkey minions helped me."

"Anger still lives, I see. But I'm impressed." His hand cupped the outrigger float.

"I don't think it's ever going to leave," I retorted, ignoring his compliment.

"It won't," Garvey said, creeping his fingers along the outrigger on the port side. "But what you need to learn is to control it. Without anger, we cannot know peace. Without hatred, we do not know love. It's about recognizing one and controlling the other."

"That sounds kind of negative," I snorted.

"It isn't. It's opposites. We cannot appreciate one thing without knowing the opposite of it. Love. Hate." He held up two fists and moved them back and forth as if they struggled for balance. "Anger. Calm." He flattened his hands, and slid them away from one another as if he smoothed out a bed sheet. Garvey's analogies made me irritable. *Anger still lives*, Garvey's words rang through my head. I hated when he was correct. Maybe my irritability was because it took me away from Juliet. She seemed to be the calm I needed. She was taming me, and we were becoming friends. It was a foreign concept, and one I'd begun to relish, but my body ached for hers. I wanted to take things deeper but didn't trust myself. Not yet. I looked off toward Juliet's tree house.

"There's a storm coming. I don't know that it will reach here, but you might want to take precautions. Tie down some things. Save up others. You haven't been fishing or gathering food like I expected."

I hadn't gone into forager mode, although after building my own boat, I imagined anything could happen next. Some moments I worried I was going native, but I had Juliet to keep me in check. She kept me sane. I don't know that I'd fare well on the island alone. She'd been my opposite. My balance.

"I'm assuming you haven't danced yet."

I rolled my eyes to the sunny sky overhead, wondering how he detected a storm from this beautiful weather.

"I don't dance alone," I said.

"Then you better summon your imaginary friend," Colton snarked. Anger certainly lived when he was near. In fact, it roared to life with his presence.

"Yeah, shut the fuck up," I snarled. It was clear he lacked balance, or he'd understand better. Imaginary or not, Juliet had become my other half.

++

I tried. I did. But dancing around the campfire was just asinine. I was a grown man, and even though no one could see me, I couldn't comprehend what I needed to discover from prancing around a circle of logs. Ironically, the trees appeared to dance as the wind picked up, and they swayed side to side. Some of them even bent gracefully backward, as if they were being dipped by a lover. I'd been taught to dance, as all young men in my social category had, so I knew the tango, the merengue, and even a salsa dance or two, but I wasn't about to dirty dance with myself.

I stalled from my attempt as a loud crackle of lightning came from up the mountain. The sky had grown dark and the stars were missing, hidden by angry clouds. Suddenly, the heavens opened and water beat down like the gods turned on a faucet. Another sharp rumble of thunder followed a second spark of lightning rippling up the sky. My thoughts immediately jumped to Juliet, and what she'd told me about her parents. She feared the lightning. While I should have taken cover into my dry tent, I raced for her tree house instead.

To my surprise, the ladder hung down as if she were expecting me. It kicked out in the increasing wind and I struggled at first to climb. The rungs were slick, and the rain was nearly sideways as if it scooped up the bay and flicked it at me. Something slammed above my head, and I hastened my climb.

"Juliet," I yelled, as I crossed onto the porch platform. It only took one large step to reach her door. I opened it against the force of the wind and slammed it behind me after I entered. Looking at the empty bed, I yelled again.

"Mouse!" My eyes quickly surveyed the small enclosure before finding her huddled on the floor near the table. Her knees were drawn up, and her head tucked against them like she'd been the night of the snake attack.

"Mouse." I breathed a sigh of relief as I squatted before her. I was soaking wet, and I reached sideways for a towel hanging over the back of a chair, swiping it over my face and my hair. She didn't look up at me.

"Hang on," I said, lifting the wet T-shirt over my head. I shifted to sit next to her, wrapping my arm around her shoulders and setting the towel over my lap.

"Come here, Mouse. We'll stay right here, but you're going to let me hold you, so you know you're safe." I gently nudged her to move forward, slipping her onto my lap. She tucked her head into my shoulder and her palm flattened on my chest. My arm curled around her lower back, resting my hand on her hip.

"I've got you," I whispered, pressing my lips to her forehead as she flinched against me after another crack and shock of light. My other hand smoothed up and down her arm.

"Want to talk?" I asked, stretching for something to distract her. She shook her head against my shoulder.

"How about we kiss?" I teased, but she shook her head again, letting out a squeak at another snapping sound outside the tree house. I momentarily thought our position in a tree might not be the safest place for us, but I didn't risk moving her. I liked that she let me hold her. I liked that I felt she needed me. I liked trying to protect her.

"Okay, baby. We'll just sit here. All night, if that's what it takes." I pressed her closer to me. Her arm snaked around my neck, and she pulled herself flush against my chest. Her face buried in the space between my neck and shoulder, and she kissed me briefly.

"Thank you," she whispered. Her appreciation pleased me. In that moment, I was more than a little prince. I was king of the jungle.

# 26

# Day 61 – Juliet

After Lillian's visit, I was shaken. My uncle had come to her for money. He'd spent all he received when my parents died—what little there had been after the sale of their home and depleting their bank account. Thoughts of him worsened my fear of lightning. I hadn't told Tack that one night I found my uncle standing at the end of my bed. The flashing light from a storm startled me awake, and I heard his heavy breathing as the thunder subsided for a moment. Holding my own breath, I deciphered the sound of skin slapping skin. I couldn't look, and my eyes twitched as another brilliant flash crossed through my window. The slick sound increased, and my heart raced as I realized what he was doing to himself. He groaned at his climax, and I swallowed back the bile in my throat.

*"Oh, Juliet. One day you'll give me everything I want from you,"* he muttered in the darkness of my room before lightning sparked again. Even after he left my room, I couldn't move, frozen with fear at the storm, his words, and his actions. After that night, I locked my room each time I went to sleep, but I didn't trust him when I was awake, either. I lived in a perpetual state of fear until I graduated high school and escaped the trailer park. I begged Lillian not to involve him in the proceedings related to the manslaughter case. Lillian said if there was any evidence I had a living relative, the experiment could be recalled. I needed a family member in case of a dead body. Even the thought of him claiming me in death made me shiver.

*"He wanted money, but this isn't a contest. You aren't winning a million dollars by surviving. This is about you and your reflective process,"* Lillian reminded me. She was correct, but the fact my uncle knew my whereabouts worried me. How could I return to Baltimore if he knew I lived there? What would happen when my time on the island was complete? Where would I go? What would become of Tack and me?

A greater question bothered me—had I atoned for my crime?

Thoughts of killing Rick niggled at me. I hadn't meant to kill Tack's friend. I hadn't thought of him like that—someone's friend, someone's son, someone's lover. But then again, Rick hadn't thought of me in that regard, and neither had Tack, until we were forced together. Could I forgive my attackers? Could I absolve them of what they did to me? In many ways, it wasn't a matter of forgiving what happened, but taking back control of my life for me. Hadn't Tack deserved that right as well? Even if I once hated him. Even if I once wished him dead, like his friend. How had everything changed? When had the shift occurred? How did I let go of the pain in order to enjoy pleasure?

I'd wrapped myself around Tack and held onto him like a life preserver, hoping to weather the storm with his strength circling me. Through the course of the night, I'd fallen asleep, despite the rumble of rain and the distancing lightning. I woke in his arms, which were slack from his sleep but still draped over my legs and around my back. I shifted, sensing he had to be uncomfortable with my weight on him all night, but his arms engulfed me and pressed me to his chest. I giggled a little.

"What's so funny?" His sleep-laden voice was rough and sexy. Something long and hard pressed against my hip. My thighs clenched and my core pulsed.

"I thought you were sleeping."

"I thought I was dreaming you in my lap," he said, roughness still in his throat as his lips pressed to my head.

"I weigh too much to sit on your lap like this," I said, pressing back on his chest, but his hands tightened on me again.

"Yet you've been here all night," he teased, his eyes still closed. "You can straddle me instead if you'd like. You know, balance out the weight and all." My head shot back, and I looked up at him to see his eyes still closed but a smirk on his face. He was teasing me without any threat. I shifted, and he groaned, the length of his excitement evident in his shorts. I shifted once again, removing the towel he had placed over his lap, and crawling over him. His eyes slowly opened.

"Keep them closed," I whispered, testing his trust. My thighs straddled either side of his. He squeezed his eyes shut but his eyebrows rose as my palms flattened on his lower abs and climbed up the ladder of his chest.

"Mouse," he croaked, as I slid forward a touch on his lap. The heat of his erection was merely a centimeter from my core. We weren't touching *there*, but the anticipation of pressure made me wet. I'd reached his shoulders and curled my palms over the bulk of them. Slowly, my hands skimmed down the length of his arms. He was still wearing my bracelet. Trapping my fingers as they drew close to his, his eyes remained closed, but they twitched. He wanted to open them and see me, but I wasn't ready.

"Not yet," I whispered. "Trust me."

"Mouse." His voice hitched, and I cut him off with the press of my lips. *I was in control*, I told myself, curling my hand around the nape of his neck. I lowered onto the length of him and he hissed against my lips. I rubbed up and down the stiff shaft beneath the heat between my thighs. Our shorts created a welcome friction. My mouth didn't leave his and I slowly sucked on his lower lip before melting both of mine to his. He took the lead with our mouths while he let me conduct the building pleasure in our laps. His mouth moved over mine, drawing me into his with deep drags. When his tongue crossed the line, I couldn't hold back any longer. I drew back, gripping his shoulders as anchors, and rolling against him. I slid my center down the heat of him, desperate to ignite us both.

"Keep that up, Mouse, and we're going to have a problem."

I nodded as my lids drifted shut. Continuing to ride him at the pace I set, I ignored his words. I was taking control of him, while his body was pleasing mine.

"Mmmm, baby, I like you taking what you want," he growled, flexing his hands on my hips. He tightly squeezed, as if to stop me. "But Mouse, we don't have to do this. We have ten months to discover one another the way we should have in the first place."

The words spurred me onward. I made no move to stop, struggling as the storm in my lower belly grew to threatening proportions. His fingers dug into my hips, and he guided our rhythm with his fingertips. The friction under the seam of my shorts grew, the tension reaching a new height as I rubbed over him, searching for relief I hadn't experienced with him yet.

"Like that, baby." It wasn't a question. He was telling me he approved of what we were doing. My mouth fell back to his but I couldn't concentrate on two areas at once. As my eruption reached its peak, my mouth hovered over his without kissing him. I groaned against his lips, drawing his breath as my oxygen because I could hardly breathe. My body tingled with relief. He captured my lips as he stilled me over him. The short jolt of his erection under me alerted me to his own release, and a moist warmth seeped between us. I felt like a vixen, as I'd cunningly taken what I wanted from him.

"You undo me," he moaned against our combined lips, still pressed to one another, but not kissing.

"I was hoping to tame you," I whispered.

"I think I want you to tame me," he hummed. "But you make me wild instead."

++

"Wait," he said, reaching for my hand and stopping me in my tracks as we traveled a new path through the jungle. I stopped, thinking he heard something or saw something. Instead, he cupped my jaw and tugged me to him, kissing me deep enough to lose my thoughts, my breath, and my whereabouts. Then he pulled back, smiling slowly as if he savored the taste on his lips, and began trekking through the trees once again, as if nothing happened, as if he hadn't just chipped away at my heart a little more.

"You seem to know your way around these woods," he said, and for some reason, a Robert Frost poem popped into my head.

"Years of practice," I grumbled. He twisted his head to glance behind at me.

"Tell me," he asked, but then looked forward again to give me the freedom to speak.

"My uncle. I told you about him and his disappointment that he inherited me. I also mentioned how inappropriate he was at times, and it became more difficult to avoid him as I grew older." I shivered with the memories. "He liked to play this game with me when I was younger and newly under his care." My memory raced backward. His voice in my head.

"He'd tell me if I could get myself out of the woods, I would be free."

"Free from what?" Tack casually asked as he walked forward. He'd missed the implication in my voice. When I didn't answer, he stopped and turned to face me. "Free from what?" His voice lowered as he looked down at me.

"I'd be free from him. If I could outrun him, I won, but if he caught me, I was his."

Tack reached forward, but let his fingers drop from my cheek moments before touching me.

"Did he ever win?" he hissed, his voice menacing and low.

"Never. I memorized those woods, making maps in my head. I always found my way out of danger." Tack continued to stare at me, his fingers flinching to comfort me, but something in my expression warned him not to touch me. "I actually think he enjoyed the chase."

I recalled my earlier memory of him standing over my bed.

*One day you'll give me everything I want from you.*

The words transposed in my head, mixing with Tack's voice. How sinister they sounded from one man. How desperate they sounded from another. He'd mentioned he wanted me to give him things. He wanted to be asked. A strange silence curled between us. Was Tack only interested in the chase with me? Or did he mean what he said? He wanted permission. We seemed to dance on the edge of a precipice, where the tiniest imbalance, either way, could crash everything.

He squeezed my hand, and we continued climbing higher up the steep mountain, passing the natural landing I'd found when I ran from him. We seemed to be traveling with our own deep thoughts as backpacks weighing down our journey.

"That looks like a cave," I announced as we came to another clearing. Spinning in a circle, I faced the great expanse of the ocean and a breathtaking view of the distant islands. It appeared as if they were only a few miles away, and in some instances, they might have been, but they were far enough to prevent escape. I turned back to find Tack entering the cave. I didn't wish to escape any longer. I didn't know how I'd leave him in ten months. Maybe the time frame sweetened the growing relationship. An end date allowed us to be as free as we wanted with one another, with no further commitment. My stomach soured at the thought.

Tack disappeared, and I hesitantly followed.

"Are bats in there? I hate bats." I groaned, ducking as I entered, even though my head was nowhere near the ceiling.

"It seems empty." His voice echoed back to me. "Just a hollowed-out niche in the side of the island. Deep enough to block out the sunlight, but it doesn't lead anywhere." I finally reached him. We were surrounded by complete darkness, with only the thinnest trickle of sunlight streaming through to us. We stood close to one another, but not touching.

"Can you hear that?" he whispered. I giggled, but as the sound softened, I tipped my head.

"It sounds like a drum." The surprising rhythm beat steadily, soothingly.

"It sounds like a heartbeat," he whispered again. He reached for my hand and tugged me against him. He didn't kiss me as he had on our walk, but his palm cupped my jaw. He seemed nervous, protective even.

"I'd never let anyone hurt you again," he said softly, suddenly, and I questioned where the words came from. Just as quickly he said, "Let's get out of here," and slipped his arm around my shoulder, guiding me to the entrance. A breeze greeted us, and off in the distance we could see clouds rolling together.

"Maybe it was just the wind, vibrating off the back of the cave," I suggested, trying to ignore the desperation in his tone.

"Maybe," he replied, but he didn't sound convinced. As we headed back in the direction we first climbed, I noticed him look over his shoulder. His brows pinched, and he shook his head before facing forward and following behind me.

+ +

We swam in the ocean. We kissed. We bathed in the pond. We kissed. We lay under the stars. We kissed. But he made no attempt to touch me deeper. I sensed he wanted to. He definitely wanted more from me, but he let me lead. We slept together most nights, taking turns at each other's dwelling, and the sexual tension grew as he held me tighter and tighter each night.

One day, we spent some time separated. I needed to focus more on my thesis, piecing together the puzzling changes in my emotions toward him. Later in the evening, I walked to his place, following a path well-worn through the jungle, but I stopped short when I saw him crawling around the fire pit. Some nights it was too hot to have a blazing bonfire, but the heat was necessary for cooking, and so the fire was lit. He circled on his hands and knees, scampering around the rocks. His head lowered as if he were sniffing the sand, and then he paused. His forehead fell into his cupped fingers and he rotated his head side to side. A giggle escaped at the strange position of his body and his head shot up.

He sprung to standing, dusting off his shorts as I approached.

"Don't laugh," he said, biting back his own smile. "It was stupid, I know." His voice lowered like a schoolboy caught doing something foolish.

"What were you doing?"

"Garvey keeps telling me I need to dance." He swiped a hand through his hair and the sand from his palm mixed with the strands growing long once again. "I thought I'd try it, though I don't understand it."

Thoughtful a moment, I stared at the divot in the sand he'd made from his crawling.

"What are you supposed to be doing…in the dance?"

"Learning something about an animal."

"What animal?" I bit my lip to prevent myself from laughing. On his hands and knees, I couldn't imagine what animal he imitated.

125

"The one I am supposed to learn from," he replied, indirectly answering me. The laughter could no longer be held back.

"It's stupid," he said, turning away from me. "Let's read or something." He took one big step toward his tent, but I reached for his wrist. Staring down at my fingers against his skin, he stopped. His eyes lifted slowly, and I saw a boy inside the man, one afraid to be laughed at, one afraid of failing.

"Try to explain it to me. What animal were you imitating?"

He sighed and looked away, swiping a hand nervously through his hair again. "A mouse." He exhaled, lowering his eyes.

"You saw a mouse on the island?" I questioned, looking around us as if I'd spot one in the sand.

"You're mocking me, aren't you?" He tugged his arm, attempting to release my grip.

"Hey," I snapped. "I'm trying to understand." He glanced up at me. "Why don't you tell me what a mouse taught you? Forget the dancing part." My fingers slipped from his wrist to his hand, loosely holding onto his fingers. His eyes shifted away.

"A mouse is small and appears helpless, but it is stronger than it seems. It's persistent. It scrambles over the ground, looking for food, seeking shelter, just trying to survive. It is determined. It is smart and it senses fear. It recognizes power." His hand reached for my jaw, a move I'd come to find affectionate in his continuous touching of me. "It's so much more than I expected." I sensed he was no longer talking about the mouse as an animal. I leaned into his palm and kissed him.

"See, unexpected." The words were rugged and low, and his throat rolled as he swallowed.

"What animal would you select?" he asked, releasing me. He stepped back and took a seat on one of the upturned stumps.

"Does it have to be an animal, or could it just be something in nature?"

"I guess it can be whatever you want it to be." He shrugged, growing bored with this concept.

"I'd choose lightning," I said. His eyes widened, but he didn't speak.

"It crackles from the earth." My feet began to stomp, and I developed a rhythm that strangely matched a song popping up in my head. "Lost on You" by LP set the tone for me, and my hips swayed in addition to my feet stomping. My hands slipped up my thighs as my hips rocked side to side.

"And the tension builds," I murmured, closing my eyes to the intensity of his stare. My fingers tickled over my belly, exposed by the tight tee that rose upward. I continued to move, skimming my flat palms upward, over my rib cage, and eventually cupping my own breasts. My eyes opened to focus on him, watching his chest rise and fall as he followed the movement of me. My palms came together and slid up my chest, rounding my neck and lacing into my hair. Raising the weight of it, I combed through the heavy locks.

"Then it breaks free." My hands released, my arms rose, fingers extended. I slowly turned in a circle, placing my back to him and continuing to move with the rhythm in my head. My hands waved above my head.

"And it illuminates the sky." My hips still swayed as my head tipped back and I looked at the darkening night rolling over us. A tempo beat in my head, encouraging the movement of my body, as I worshipped the sky above me. I was lost to myself for a moment—the cool sand at my feet, the midnight sky over my head.

"What did you learn from the lightning, though?" His voice was directly behind me, but he didn't startle me. In fact, I felt his presence but refused to let it break the spell I was under. I wanted him to join me instead.

"I learned that even something as dangerous as lightning can be beautiful," I whispered out to the ocean before me. "And even lightning has a weakness. It cannot be alone. Thunder always works in tandem with it." Hands gripped my hips, and the heat of his body pressed behind mine. He joined my rhythm, his hips matching the sway of mine, and as one, we danced. If I closed my eyes, I could pretend we were at a night club. Perhaps The Front Door, on the dance floor, surrounded by a sea of people, where the only two that existed for us was the two of us. But I didn't want to close my eyes. I didn't need to pretend. It was only us, along the shore of the ocean, the stars our spotlight, and we danced without a care.

He spun me to face him without missing a beat and increased the exaggerated tempo as if a DJ set a sultry, pulsating beat. He guided my body to move with his as his hands climbed from my hips to the sides of my breasts. He skimmed under my arms, out to my fingers, and in one smooth move, spun me away from him. Then he tugged me back, gyrating in a way that rivaled dirty dancing. I could have giggled in my awkwardness. I wasn't one for public dancing, but this was Tack, and I gave in to him. Lost on him. He was fully engrossed in our dancing, rolling my hips to match his. Dragging my thigh upward, the dance had taken a new direction. He dipped me backward, kissed my throat and slowly lifted me. He moved us as one, released me again to spin away from him and then curled me back against his chest. We ended in the same position we started, my back to his front, and we swayed as he nibbled at my neck.

"Come inside the tent with me." His voice turned husky. "Please." The intention in that single word was clear. He was asking, and I could deny him, but I didn't want to. I nodded to agree.

"I promise I'll be gentle. We'll go at your pace," he whispered into my skin. I twisted to look up at him over my shoulder before reaching for his hand and stepping away from him. I walked backward, guiding him with each labored step on the soft sand. Reaching the open tent flaps, I ducked and led us inside. His pallet was on the ground, and I released his hand to climb to the center of his mattress. His eyes didn't leave mine, and I tugged off my tight T-shirt.

"Sweet Jesus, Mouse." It wasn't like he hadn't seen me naked before, but his eyes swallowed the heavy weight of my breasts peeking out the top of my bra. He fell to his knees, jostling the mattress, and stripped off his own tee. "This okay?" he asked, but the desperate look in his eyes begged me to agree. "I want to be close to you, Juliet."

I nodded, and he leaned forward to kiss me, taking his time to trace over my lips with his own, and then added his tongue to memorize the curl and curve. I sucked at him until his mouth became one with mine and I found myself pressed back to lay on his cool sheet. A breeze blew in from the open flaps and the air was refreshing. His hand hesitated at my waist before traveling upward and cupping one of my breasts over my bra. I moaned into his mouth as he squeezed and then slipped a finger under the cotton material. The tip of his finger flicked over the sharp peak of my nipple, and he broke the kiss.

"Let me take this off." His statement was a question, a commanding plea. I nodded, and he nearly sighed with relief as his hand slipped behind my back and removed the clasps. Dragging the material forward, achy breasts fell, nipples standing at attention with the soft breeze. He took a moment to knead each one of them before dropping his mouth to latch onto one at a time. He sucked and he tugged, and my hips rose in search of his lower body. His palm lowered to the waist of my shorts, fumbling with the button while his mouth distracted me. Then he kissed a trail of sucking kisses and sliding tongue over my belly to the edge of my shorts.

"Please, Mouse." He blew air onto my lower abdomen as he hesitated for my permission. My hands came to the side of my shorts and pushed them downward, giving him his answer. He completed the rest of the removal, taking my underwear with them. I lay naked in more ways than one before him, and he sat back on his calves to take in the view. The breeze blew up my open legs and the air tickled, adding to the pulsing need between my thighs.

"You're so beautiful, Mouse, all spread out and waiting for me. I don't know where to start. I want to please you in so many ways." He didn't wait for an answer as his hands massaged up my thighs and tugged my legs further apart. Fingers found their way to slick skin.

"You're so wet already. Do you want me?" The betrayal of my body proved I did, but the question felt deeper. I could only nod, and the answer awarded me a thick digit thrusting forward. I sighed in pleasure, my thighs coming together to hold him in place. His free hand pushed them apart and the cool ocean air whirled between my legs. I moaned.

"Feel the air? You like that, don't you?" I couldn't speak. "Even the air wants to taste you." The thought left me breathless, feeling light and one with nature. Sometimes, I felt as if I was part of the island, and this was one of those moments. He added another finger, and my thoughts muddled. It was only the soft wind, his warm skin, and the slickness between my thighs. My hips rolled, sucking him into me, clenching as he twirled inside me. With the addition of his thumb on my sensitive nub, I came hard and saw stars. An animalistic groan released as if telling the island, I ruled this land. His touch made me feel like a queen.

He parted my knees with his own slipping between mine, and my languid body panicked for a second.

"One more," he whispered, lowering his head, and his mouth covered sensitive skin already wet and ready. He sucked at tender folds, twirled his tongue through my slit and parted me in a way I'd never been touched before. My fingers combed through his hair as my head fell back on his pillow. My body was no longer my own, but his to do as he pleased. My hips curled and my thighs fell further open. One of his hands slipped under my knee, holding me spread for his pleasure. He lapped at my core, making soft noises, as my body tremored, another quake rising, ready to break. I screamed at the release, lifting my head and pressing hands into his hair. His tongue didn't stop until I cried out that I couldn't take any more. He flattened it for a final lap and then kissed my inner thigh. The removal of his head brought cool air swirling up my legs, and my center pulsed again. Death by orgasm became a sudden fear.

"I want you so much, Mouse," he said to my open core, and I clenched with the thought. His fingers traced lazy circles around my clit, building a slow tension, and my lower body reacted as if it wanted to reach for him and draw him in. "It's building again, isn't it?" He marveled at where his fingers touched me, and blew at my tender skin, adding heat to the cool sensation of the natural breeze. My head rolled on the pillow but I had no words.

Without missing a beat, he pushed down his own shorts, never releasing the finger touching me. He crawled between my thighs, gripping the sharp length of him between his hand, and holding his head at my entrance, slipping it up and down.

"Let me in," he whispered, but I didn't reply. He looked up at me, focused on my eyes. He must have seen something missing, something he didn't like, because instead, he slipped over my legs to rest at my side. I wasn't ready for more than this, and without realizing I had tensed, I relaxed. He returned his finger to his previous attention, and my hand hesitated to touch him. I'd gripped him before, allowing him to lead me in stroking him, but this time I wanted to explore. My fingers tickled up the stiff shaft, rising and dipping with each ripple along the taut skin. The smoothness of his head seeped with liquid, and I spread it over him, using it to moisten the tip and cover my palm. I cupped his heavy sac, squeezing them in my hand before encircling the heavy length of him again. In a slow jerking motion, I worked over him while he circled my core and the wind licked my lower lips. I came once again with a soft cry and squeezed him harder.

"Like that, baby," he muttered, releasing my body to lay back and let me control his. I shifted hands, tipping up on an elbow and watched as I stroked him. It wasn't fast enough. It wasn't hard enough, and my body hummed for command. I knelt and straddled his thigh, lowering my lips to kiss the tip.

"Fuck, Mouse," he mumbled, a string of additional curses and pleas followed as his hand lazily combed through my loosening hair. My lips opened, and I slid down the length of him, letting my tongue lap over those tight ridges before drawing him deeper. I sucked him to the back of my throat and then worked my way back up to the tip.

"Again," he hissed, and his leg shook between my knees. I pressed my wet core over his thick thigh and lay across him, my breasts straddling him as well. My mouth swallowed him, and I sucked at the thickness until he cried out, pulsing at the back of my throat. I released him slowly, my tongue lingering as it drifted upward until he called out with a chuckle, "Enough."

Instantly, his arms circled me, and he dragged me level with him on his bed. His body lay half over mine, his face in my neck, his breath tickling. I felt his heart racing over my arm, and my free hand reached for his hair. Combing upward through the soft locks, I massaged at his skull.

"Don't ever leave me, Mouse," he muttered, his voice lazy and satisfied. The comment gave me thought—ten months remaining might not be enough time.

# 27

# Day 67 – Tack

I woke with her under me, shocked that we hadn't shifted in our sleep. She amazed me. I didn't feel her forgiveness, but I felt her letting me in. Slowly. Carefully. Deeply. I was getting under her skin as much as she was getting beneath mine.

"Good morning," she whispered, her voice husky with sleep.

"Good morning," I sighed, nibbling at her neck. I didn't typically spend the full night with a woman, but I'd spent many with Juliet. I liked knowing she was next to me. I'd stopped thinking she was a dream and started accepting her as my reality. We had so much to do, so much to learn, but we were taking steps in the right direction.

"What's that sound?" she said. I hadn't heard anything and I chuckled.

"I think it's my stomach," I muttered into her sleep-warm skin. "I'm hungry." I was starving, but more so, I was famished for her. I wanted second helpings of everything. Moments like this. Days spent together. Nights taking things further. I couldn't say how far we'd get, but we had months to work things out. Neither of us was going anywhere soon, and there was a certain comfort in that thought.

"It sounds like something's gurgling. Like a fizzing noise."

I leaned up on my elbow and a finger traced down the middle of her body, between the valley of her breasts, the flatland of her belly and leading to the bush at the top of her legs. Her hand stopped my journey.

"Tack." I looked down at her. "I'm serious."

One tent flap was snapping in the wind. We'd fallen asleep with the tent wide open, and surprisingly, we hadn't had any visitors. Originally, I had no intention of sharing my things with the wildlife, but how different I felt after two months. I stood to close the flap, assuming it was the noise she heard, when I saw a thin wave of water rush up to the fire circle. Watching the water recede, I noticed the tide had come much closer to the dwelling. More importantly, the waves had begun to crest and crash in a more riotous motion against the beach. The sky was gray—solid gray—which is something we hadn't seen. Most rain clouds filled and passed easily over the island with blue skies leading the path and trailing behind. This was different. This was a tropical storm.

"Shit," I hissed, turning back to her, still spread naked over my mattress. I wanted nothing more than to open her and take my time to explore again, but we had more pressing matters. "I think a storm is coming. A big one. Could you help me tie stuff down?"

She sat up and an arm crossed her chest as if that would cover her. I stalked back to the bed.

"Let's hope it's nothing, but it might be better to pull up my camp and move some things to your place."

Her eyes opened wide and she nodded. Then she scrambled off the bed and began dressing. I didn't want to panic her, but the more I listened to the sound of the waves and the increase in the wind, the more the change in weather hinted at something stronger than a storm. We worked diligently. She collected most of my loose items: pots and pans, coffee pot, the hammock, and placed them in one of my four trunks. While my tent was just inside the jungle edge, the trunks were further back for safe keeping. One stored food. Another was my clothing. Two were full of camp supplies. I dismantled the tent as best I could and dumped it in a relatively empty trunk.

"I think it might be best if I try to tie these to a tree or two." The way the water was climbing the beach, I didn't know how far it would reach, but I didn't need my things floating out to sea. I rolled my sleeping bag and tucked it in a backpack along with a random assortment of clothing and the copy of *The Little Prince*. I threw in a propane tank, matches, and a lantern. I'd once had to fill out a survival guide in high school. *Rank the items you'd need to survive.* I couldn't think as a kid, but looking up at Juliet, a strange thought occurred. I decided there wasn't anything else I'd need but her.

She watched as I tied a fisherman's knot on the handle of each trunk. Another skill I hadn't used in a while, despite my previous interest in tying willing women to beds. I hadn't thought of that possibility, those women, for months, and I looked up again to find Juliet staring at me. Panic set in her eyes, panic I recognized. She was frightened, but I'd do anything to assure her we were safe. My own heart raced, but I swallowed down my fear. I finished quickly and approached her.

"I won't let anything happen to you," I said before kissing her forehead. She nodded against my lips. Without words, I didn't know if she fully trusted me, but I was all she had at the moment, and we were about to face something we hadn't had to deal with yet: nature and its wrath.

+ +

Inside her tree house, I used binoculars to try to see the ocean. I didn't have a view of my beach and had no idea how my things were fairing. Besides, the rain was coming sideways again, appearing almost like a white sheet, making visibility impossible.

"The waves are increasing," I stated. I didn't like the sound of the wind rustling the trees. The whistling sound was increasing, an extreme sort of white noise, that was grating on my nerves. The subtle crack and snap of smaller limbs around us alerted us to the strength of the gusts. I wasn't convinced we were safe in her tree house. Water couldn't get us here, so I didn't worry as much about flooding, but if the gale force picked up a few levels, we'd be blown out like the leaves.

"I think we should seek higher ground. Maybe sturdier shelter." I spun to face her. She'd been sitting on the edge of her bed, chewing a nail, which I hadn't seen her do before. Her violet eyes were too wide and her knee jiggled.

I called her name and her attention snapped up to me. "I think we need to find that cave."

She nodded but she hadn't moved. A gust of wind shook the tree limbs over the low roof over our heads and she understood. The roof creaked, a strange strain on the boards, as if something were tugging at them to be free. We couldn't stay where we were.

"Pack some clothes. Maybe your blanket. I have my sleeping bag." I scanned her room. "Collect your notes." I knew she'd been working hard to compose her thoughts each day on the island and I didn't want her to lose all that work. She digested her feelings much better than me. I'd only worked up to three or four sentences a day in my journaling, while she had filled pages.

She collected her notebooks in a satchel bag and then filled a backpack with her blanket and a few clothes. I filled a second backpack with water bottles and any foods I thought we could survive on for a few days. A tropical storm could last twenty-four hours or longer. On an island as small as ours, I could only hope the clouds would pass quickly but with nothing but the sea around us, the weather could decide to stay and play, spiraling around us instead of moving onward.

The second we opened her door and struggled to lift the hatch for her ladder we were in for a battle. The stairs floated through the harsh air.

"I'll go first so we'll climb down together. I know the ropes can't really hold us both, but I don't want to lose you. We'll just work as fast as we can." She was so lightweight, I feared she'd blow away. "You'll have to trust me." Her wide eyes flashed to mine, but her focus was missing. Again, I had that sense that she didn't have faith in me, but she had to believe I would do what I could to keep us safe.

I stepped down a few rungs and then reached for her. "Trust me." I sought her eyes to assure her. She turned her body so her back was to me and filled in the limited space above me. My hand came to her hip to guide her descent, reinforcing that I was here for her. As the ladder resisted, attempting to fly sideways, our climb strained the rope linking, but I didn't want to lose a hold on her. The descent seemed slow and we struggled with each rung as the ladder flung us nearly sideways. I didn't dare release my hold on her, moving my fingers to her belt. Finally, we hit the ground.

"If we stay low, and rush through the brush, it might protect us a little." I didn't intend for us to crawl, but we had to stay hunched over, protecting our heads from the slapping tree limbs and using them to shield us from the wind. The rain pelted just as fierce, stinging as we slipped over the muddy earth. The upward climb was even more of a struggle than I expected, and at times I felt like I was dragging Juliet. She didn't complain, but she tugged at me, resisting me. The climb grew steeper. Every moment I thought we were closer, we weren't. I worried I miscalculated where we found the cave.

"I don't know where it is," I yelled, my words carried off in the gusty air. If she heard me, she didn't answer, just clutched my hand, as if all her trust laid in that connection.

We continued on, with the wind beating our backs and twigs smacking our body. At one point, Juliet released me, and I spun, afraid she wouldn't still be behind me. With her eyes closed, her hands cupped her forehead. She stepped back, and I feared she'd slide down the steep slope. I reached for the strap of her satchel and pulled her forward.

"What happened?" I shouted.

"My head." Releasing her hands, a gash across her forehead was all I needed to know. I reached out as if I would pick her up, but she pushed me away. "You can't carry me. Keep going."

Her voice filtered through the howling gale, the sound haunting. I pushed her before me and forced her forward with me at her back. If she passed out, at least I could catch her.

Eventually, we broke through the bushes, reaching the flat landing before the cave. As Juliet stepped first, the wind took her sideways. My heart left my body as I envisioned her thrown from the cliff ledge, and I reached for the strap of her bag again. Tugging her down to the moss-covered rocks, we crawled to the cave entrance. I hadn't given a thought to animals or other critters finding shelter from the weather within the hollow. They would have to share the space because I wasn't going back down the mountain.

We burst through the entrance and Juliet immediately sat with her back to the rock wall. I passed her, scrambling to stand, as I searched our surroundings as best I could in the dim light. My knees gave way and I began searching for the propane lantern. I couldn't let it run all night, but we needed to see the inside of the cave and warm up a little bit. Plus, I wanted to inspect Juliet's forehead. We hadn't thought to bring a first-aid kit.

"Mouse," I hollered. The tapping of her crawling behind me told me she followed my command. Shaky fingers struck a match and lit the wick of the propane tank. The cave illuminated, and to my relief, nothing else hid within. The cavern's walls were the purest black I'd ever seen, slick with a sheen, but brilliant and dry.

"Here." I walked on my knees and opened my sleeping bag, spreading it wide against the back wall. I directed Juliet to follow. She hadn't made a sound and I worried she'd gone into shock or had a concussion. "Let me look, Mouse." She shivered before me, and I noticed her clothing was soaked, as was mine. I didn't know what was worse—the sting of the rain or the slap of the wind.

"Let me see your head." Tenderly I caressed over the cut, and she flinched. I reached for my shirt, tugged it over my head and dabbed at the blood. The tree raked over her skin, leaving a gash that didn't look deep but was long. She still hadn't made a noise, and her silence frightened me.

Inside the cave, the haunting howl dissipated. Tucked back into a corner, we were protected from the elements. Neither the wind nor the rain could reach us here or so I hoped. Juliet continued to shiver next to me. We were facing a long night trying to survive a hurricane. With no weather warning system, no cell phone, or emergency radio, we had not been prepared, and my anger grew with the thought, especially when I envisioned Juliet blowing off that ledge. Garvey had told me a storm was coming, but this wasn't what I expected. And there was nothing he could do to help me. Juliet and I had to figure it out, together.

"We need to get out of these wet clothes." I'd already removed my shirt and began taking off my shorts. Juliet hadn't moved. "Mouse, take off your wet things."

She didn't look up, her body trembling.

"Mouse?" I questioned, reaching for her shirt and slowly unbuttoning it. Her eyes had lost their focus and stared into emptiness, definitely shock of some type. "I need to warm you up." Though it had been humid, the rain soaked us to the core and my teeth chattered with a chill. She still hadn't moved, and my patience was thinning. The rush of adrenaline still coursed through my body.

"Mouse, take off your clothes," I snapped. "We need our body heat to warm each other." Her head slowly lifted, but she made no attempt to follow my directions. Shaking with the need to be close to her, and the surge of adrenaline, I barked at her again.

"We're going to play this my way. Blink if you understand me."

# 28
## The Island Touches Your Heart

Her eyes blinked with the recognition of those fateful words, the ones he spoke in an attempt to protect her. The only words he used to try to get her out of a terrible situation. He was a decent man who had made a bad decision. He hadn't been cruel, like the other man. In fact, she couldn't recall him being rough at all. His eyes had struck her. For a moment, he looked repentant. He seemed to be asking her something. Generally, his presence suggested he wasn't one to ask, but in this instance, he wanted something of her. And then it passed, and he whispered those words over her mouth, gagged and unwilling. His lips covered hers.

His body shielded hers, but she'd turned numb. So cold, she thought. Resigned to a worse fate, she lay there, waiting for the second intrusion, an invasion that never came. He brushed back her hair, and the weight of him rested between her thighs, but he hadn't entered her. She'd remember if he had, she decided. She'd remember him like that.

Presently, she heard the ripping of buttons off a shirt and warm hands pushing back damp clothing. *So wet*, she thought. Palms rubbed up and down her cold skin, and her body jostled with the roughness of his touch.

"Mouse," he whispered harshly and she looked up at him, recalling who he was and who he'd become. He was caring for her once again. He cared about her, she decided. His mouth descended over hers, and the instant it connected, she flared back to life. Her arms wrapped around his neck, and she pulled him to her. They tumbled back onto the makeshift bed.

"Clothes off," he commanded, and she wrestled with her own shorts and underwear as he removed his. They sighed in unison when they came back together, the heat of skin and the warmth of bodies, igniting the other. Hands explored. Fingers caressed. Mouths melded as one.

"Let me in," he pleaded. His lips covered her skin over her racing heart. Her thighs opened, allowing him entrance to a foreign land. The tip of him spread her, and he sailed forward. The sensation filled the dark cavern with a collective moan of relief.

He would be gentle with her. He would be patient. He would be kind. He was like a wave, rolling forward, crashing against her shore, and like the wet sand on the beach, she followed each retreat, waiting for the rush to happen again. They continued this pattern of him curling over her and her tumbling under him until the friction became too much. Like the angry sea surrounding the island, the rhythm increased, becoming a collision of crashing ocean and soft sand.

"Mouse," he struggled, questioning the sensation. Her hands reached for his firm backside, and he lifted her knee, drawing himself deeper, wanting to drown in her.

She dug her fingers into the solid globes of his rear and clenched her thighs at his waist. Her groans murmured off the walls of the cave, where she asked to be tamed and claimed and owned by him. Rushing as she came, the orgasm didn't want to subside as another wave developed, and he rode her faster. He balanced over her, towering up on two hands. She'd become the island, letting the ocean take her and the wind claim her, and his thrusting increased as she climbed upward, chasing another release that would wreck her.

"I love you," she screamed as the storm of him pounded against her. He stilled. The words stunned him, but she didn't think to worry. She was coming again, a river of rushing emotion as her body was wrapped around him, and then the subtle pulse of him inside her, beats of his own release, filled her.

"What did you say?" he asked through clenched teeth. The sound wasn't angry. He was confused, lost in the question. His eyes glistened.

A shaky hand wiped sweat at his brow, bodies still connected as one.

"I love you," she whispered, one part fearing his wrath, and the other part bold enough to admit the emotion.

She loved him when she once hated him.

"Don't say that," his voice trembled, liquid threatening to leak from his eyes. "Don't say that unless you mean it." His eyes closed, shutting off the tunnel to his emotions.

"I love you," she repeated. "You have tamed me. I am a part of you, and you are a part of me. You make me feel unique and I—"

His mouth crushed hers, at first intense and almost bruising. She thought he wanted to stop her and yet he wanted to draw her in, taste the words and devour them. Like a child with a treat he'd never experienced, he couldn't get enough of her sweetness.

He pulled back almost as abruptly as he claimed her lips. His palm pushed back the sweaty hair on her forehead.

"I didn't know it felt like this," he said, his voice catching. "I didn't think *I* could feel like this. You make me wild." He inhaled as he rolled, flipping her over him. Then he exhaled as he began the slow pleasure of filling her again. He hardened inside her as he lowered and lifted her by her hips. He watched them move in unison, taking his fill of entering her and disappearing deep into her cavern. An intoxicating scent filled the cave, fragranced with the scent of sex and the aroma of love. This was a den of bodily homage, and he worshipped her in his own way. The thrusting increased quickly, her body reacting with jolts and jiggles over his.

"You make me wild," he said, bucking upward, as she slammed down on him. "I love you," he choked, the words foreign and sweet to his lips. "And I'm sorry."

"Tack," she questioned, trying to slow the rhythm, but his hands controlled her. His body dominated. He forced her to keep pace and follow his lead.

"I'm sorry, I'm sorry, I'm sorry," he grunted and sat up a bit, reaching for her lips. Kissing aggressively, his mouth sucked at hers. He pressed firmly against her lips, forcing her to feel his sorrow as he spoke, "I love you, I love you, I love you."

Then he fell back and his hips forced her upward. Her hands came to his chest to steady herself, holding on through the storm of him. His heart raced beneath her touch. He burst inside her, a volcanic eruption leaving him replete, and a rush of wetness escaped down her thighs. His hand came to her lower belly as he stilled, and his thumb slipped to the bundle of nerves aching to be triggered. Several firm circles and she erupted over him, rolling over his lowering length like the clouds chasing one another in the sky. She came softly, sweetly, deeply. There was no other way to describe it. She showered him tenderly with the curl of her hips, allowing her warmth to surround him, and emotions to be released in another gentle cry of love. She fell forward, collapsing on his chest. A limp arm came over her back as they folded into one another. Using his heart beat as her pillow, she fell into a deep sleep, content with his apology and his love.

# 29

# Day 69 – Juliet

We awoke slowly and made love a second time in the night, ignoring the potential danger outside the cave. There seemed to be a sense of urgency to our love making. His plea had snapped me out of my shock. His apology unleashed my emotions. His love made each touch that much more special. We explored with frenzied hands and hungry mouths during the second round, and just when I thought I was satisfied, I'd find I was starving for him again. It was as if we knew the time in the cave was limited, and we didn't wish to rest. While we both wanted to stay forever, the storm would subside, the day would break, and reality would return. Only we couldn't have predicted how quickly.

Tack scoped out the damage, returning to inform me the sun was shining. While the sky still looked angry in the distance, we were surrounded in blue calm.

"I think we need to go down and assess what remains." He said the words in a business manner, and I had a brief glimpse of the tycoon he was, but then his mouth took mine again. We kissed, a desperate work of his lips molding and sculpting mine. His hand cupped my jaw in that tender, protective way he had, and I savored his touch, his kiss, and the way his body connected with mine.

"I just can't get enough of you," he added, whispering the words close to my lips so I could taste them, inhale them. I was high on him, intoxicated by what we'd done the night before. The thought of him filling me made me wet and longing.

"How's your head?" I hadn't given it a thought. A thick scab formed to protect my skin from the nasty gash I'd felt with my fingers the night before. Tracing over it with his finger, he reached forward and tenderly kissed a path over it. "You're beautiful," he assured me, in spite of the fact we both knew it might scar.

He rolled away from me, taking his warmth and his nakedness. I stared after him, admiring his body that fit with mine in a way I didn't think any man's body ever would. He'd been gentle while eager, passionate while savage. He nipped, and sucked, and licked me everywhere. I shivered at the thought. I watched him dress, and then took the hint to cover myself, thankful we each had a clean, dry set of clothing. We packed up our belongings. With each motion, each item, a slow sadness sank within me. Disappointment wasn't the word. Grief, possibly. Something big, monumental, seemed over, and I couldn't shake the growing dread. *It's nothing*, I told myself. We still had months together, but as we crossed the entrance to the cave and slowly descended the rocks, the sensation pressed heavier than the wind from the storm.

Trees were scattered—some broken while others remained unscathed. We had to climb over a few fallen ones, and skate carefully down muddy paths using loose limbs to guide us.

We'd just reached another large trunk crossing our path when a call came up the mountain.

"Juliet." My name rose distant and weak, but definite. Tack and I both froze before the fallen tree.

"Lillian?" I questioned softly, my heart suddenly racing. They'd come for me, but they were early. I turned to Tack, his eyes wide, worried, and questioning. He stepped toward me and cupped my chin.

"They've come because of the storm," I said to assure both him and me. Our fifteen-day visit wasn't due for a few more days.

"I'm not ready," he said, his eyes searching mine before his mouth crushed my lips. Our teeth actually clashed as the force was so intense. I struggled under his hold, groaning his name against his mouth.

"Just one," he whispered, pulling back briefly and then returning to my mouth with his, gentler this time. Tears sprang behind my closed lids. *Just one what?* I thought.

He answered me with his manner. His hands began to fumble with the buttons at my shirt. His other hand reached for my shorts.

"My way," he muttered against my lips. "Just once." The words were aggressive, said through clenched teeth, but I didn't fear him. I swallowed his fear instead. Something bothered him, and his body

144

vibrated with the same tension I'd felt while packing our things. My hands covered his cheeks, and I tugged his mouth to mine. He pulled back and spun me.

"Hands on the log," he demanded, and I did as he said, letting him command me with his need. My shorts were tugged to the ground and his hand slipped inside my open shirt, digging under tank and bra for skin. His fingers found my nipple and pinched while he fumbled with his own shorts behind me. The clank of a belt. The rip of a zipper. Warm length pressed against my cool ass.

"I love you," he murmured into my neck, and I was overcome with sensation. Two fingers rolled my nipple, one finger parted my folds, and suddenly he entered me without warning. I lunged forward a bit, my elbows breaking my balance.

"Sweet Jesus," he muttered as his hands gripped my hips, and he tugged me back while he pushed forward, pressing deeper into me than I'd ever felt someone before. "You have no idea how beautiful you look like this. Drawing me in. You've opened for me, let me in, and I can't let you go." His voice cracked and I tried to look over my shoulder, but the insistent hammering distracted me, forcing me to face forward. A hand slipped between my thighs, then traveled upward for the pearl of flesh he liked to circle.

"Don't scream," he warned, knowing I could be loud, and they'd hear me from below. *They were here.* The thought seemed to come to us collectively as he thrust faster, harder, deeper, and I pressed back, drawing him in, clutching at his length, begging him with my body to stay attached to me. *Don't let me go,* I whispered through sharp exhalations, but no sound escaped my lips.

"Mouse," he warned, as he increased the pace, thrusting into me while his thumb played with me. I crashed, my knees buckling, as the release came from deep inside me. He pressed me forward and my arms draped over the thick trunk. The angle shifted the depth of him and he slid through heavy wetness before forcing me forward with the thrust of his stillness. He leaned over my back, pressing his forehead to my shoulder blade as he pulsed inside me and I reveled in the aftershocks of his release.

"I love you," he kissed over my back.

"I love you," I said through harried breaths. The words seemed a farewell.

++

"Let me go with you," he said, as we descended the mountain. We drew closer to the tree house, but still distant enough we couldn't be seen yet. The cries of my name grew louder, more insistent, and spreading as Lillian seemed to travel in one direction and Franco in the other.

"I haven't ever mentioned you to Lillian. I don't think she would receive it well if you suddenly showed up with me. I'll be okay. Let me go down to them and then I'll come find you after they leave." We had stopped walking as he paused us with his hand on my arm. He stepped closer to me.

"I don't like this."

I shrugged. "They've only come to check on me. Make sure I survived the storm." I tipped up on my toes and kissed him briefly.

"I'll find you," I said, pushing back on his chest as I took a step backward. In that moment, I memorized his face for some reason. Moss green eyes alight with concern, sparkled with something I hadn't noticed before in them. His skin was tan, and his lips full from our kissing. He licked at the bottom one and sucked it in, exposing a hint of his white teeth. He reached out for me again, catching my arm and tugging me back to him for another soul-rocking kiss. His mouth was my heaven, and I smiled at the thought, with my lips over his. He let me go, joining my smile, his expression confirming we shared a secret.

"I'll find you," I said again, waved once and turned for the brush.

"I'll be waiting," he whispered. His eyes pressed on my back until I disappeared. It was as if I felt the exact moment he could no longer see me. I took a deep breath.

"Lillian," I called out, feeling my heart collapse with grief.

# 30

## Day 69 – Tack

I waited until I could no longer see her and then I turned for my camp. I didn't expect much to remain. If the waves crashed the land like I anticipated, there was a high possibility most of my things washed away. I trudged over the wrecked land of crushed small trees and snapped trunks perched against others for support. I neared the pond and took a moment to pause, admiring how it seemed unscathed. The waterfall still fell, although the pond looked fuller. The water was clear of color and a vision of Juliet on that first day I saw her came to my mind. An ache in my chest pressed me forward.

I cleared the low brush near the shore, and to my surprise, I found Colton staring at the water and Garvey pacing the sand. The ocean still collided on the beach, but the waves were gentler than the days before. The speed boat that brought me here rocked where it was anchored.

Garvey sighed as he spun in his pacing and froze when he saw me. "Thank God," he barked. Colton looked up from his spot, kicking the sand at his feet.

"How are my things?" I asked, walking toward my trunks.

"How are you?" Colton asked, a strange sound of relief in his question.

"I'm fine," I said, too calm, too easily. The two men glanced at one another and looked back at me.

"You just survived a hurricane," Colton stated as if I didn't know the depth of severity that storm brought to the island. I shrugged as I walked forward. Only two trunks remained tied to trees. I spun slowly, taking in the beach as if I expected the other trunks to magically appear or be found somewhere among the rocks lining the bay.

"*The Vixen*," I sighed, noticing immediately that my craft was gone. I should have known better. Although I tried to tie it to a tree, made of simple bark and saplings, the wind alone might have ripped it from its holding.

"The what?" Colton asked.

"My boat," I answered, a touch of sadness that my hard work and the work shared with Juliet had been washed out to sea.

"You guys are early," I added, attempting to change the subject as I stood before one trunk, unsnapping the locks, ready to assess the internal damage. The lid was only partially raised when Garvey spoke.

"We're here to remove you."

"What?" The lid released from my hold and fell with a snap against the case. I spun to face them. "My time isn't finished." Panic filled my voice. Juliet raced through my mind.

"There's another hurricane coming within a day or two. Now is our window to get you back to a bigger island, possibly to the mainland."

"But I don't want to go," I said, stepping forward. This caused Colton to glance at his father again.

"Why not?" the elder asked.

"I'm not ready," I said, lowering my tone. "I didn't finish my sentence."

"You've finished it, as far as we are concerned. The trial didn't include putting you at risk of death. A hurricane is beyond the means of danger." Garvey walked past me toward one end of the closest trunk. He nodded at his son who stepped forward to the other side.

"Wait," I said, holding out my hands, one toward each of them. I stepped in front of the case, blocking the removal of my things. "There's a cave. Up the mountain. That's where I was. It's safe there."

"Sorry, Champ," Garvey said, "but our orders are to bring you home."

"Whose orders?" I asked, suspicious.

"Your father's."

"No." I sounded like a petulant child.

"The authorities agree."

"I'm not going to jail," I snapped.

"Your sentence has been reassessed due to the circumstances." Garvey paused examining my face. "What's really going on here?" he asked, his hand releasing my trunk and his hands coming to rest on his hips. His dark eyes pierced mine with the question.

"It's the girl, isn't it?" Colton hissed.

"Colton," Garvey warned his son, and my attention swung from father to son and back.

"Fine," I said, swiping a hand through my hair. "It's the girl. She's here, and I'm not leaving without her." The world seemed to stop moving. The air stilled. Even the ocean didn't roll.

"She gave this to me." I held up my wrist. "And she helped me build the boat." I looked over Garvey's shoulder, a brief glimpse of us working together to create something. "And I danced." I stepped toward him.

"I danced. And she danced with me. She taught me, and I learned about a mouse."

"A mouse?" Colton snickered as Garvey continued to stare.

"She…she loves me," I said softer, directly to Garvey, begging him to hear me.

Instead, he reached for the edge of my trunk once again, ignoring my outburst. Without another thought, I turned and ran. I sprinted through the bush, leaping over fallen branches, racing for the tree house. My heart thumped as my chest filled with air and fear. I pressed harder, moved faster, crossing the line to the space surrounding her tree.

Nothing remained as it had been.

The tree house was in two pieces. One-half still clung to the tree, open and exposed to the elements. Long vines and thick branches dangled before it. The other half had crashed to the ground, crushed into a pile prepared for a bonfire. More vines draped over it and a fallen tree pressed it further into the damp jungle floor. I stopped and stared, my chest rising and falling with exertion, and something more. Something deeper that pierced and pinched and rolled my stomach.

"Juliet," I said softly, afraid I'd wake the sleeping tree and the fallen house.

"Mouse," I choked louder just as Colton burst through the brush behind me. He came to stand next to me, his breaths coming heavy, his hands holding his sides. I didn't move my eyes from the tree house.

"She's not here," he said softly, almost kindly, as if he understood.

"She was," I said quietly, while he stared at the wreck before us. "She was," I said louder, my heart leaping up to my throat as I took in the broken structure.

"The storm," I muttered.

"This damage is older than a storm, my friend." His voice was gentle, but the tenderness pissed me off.

"She was here," I insisted, turning to face him. I reached for his shirt and tugged him toward me. "She was here," I growled.

"I know you want to believe it," he said calmly. "I know," he emphasized.

"You know nothing," I yelled in his face, holding him against me.

"I know that you hurt her, and you're sorry. You want it to be okay, but it can never be. She wasn't here, man. *I know* you want her to be here. You want to make it right, but you can't. She wasn't here." His voice lowered, and I released him with a shove.

"Shut up," I said through clenched teeth. "Shut the fuck up." *She left*, I told myself. She went with Lillian. Conflicting thoughts rolled through my head. Excuses. Explanations. *She was safe*, I argued. *Please let her be safe*, I prayed.

"I didn't dream her," I said, assuring both myself and Colton.

"You did. She was beautiful, right? She was perfect, yeah? She forgave you." His voice thickened. I turned to face him.

"What do you know?" I hissed. *She loves me*, I screamed in my head.

"She loved you," he repeated as if he heard my thoughts. "But it wasn't real."

"Stop it," I yelled, covering my ears like a child.

"I know what you're feeling. I've been here before." He nodded in the direction of the fallen haven. "I wanted to believe it, too. But it wasn't real. She was already gone. She couldn't have been here." His voice drifted off as if in a memory, and I stared at him, mouth falling open.

"What happened?" I whispered.

"I did something that could never be repaired. Not with her. Coming here gave me focus—clarity and perspective—but I could never be fully restored. I couldn't bring her back." He sucked in air on the words and closed his eyes. He was silent a second, and I turned back to the pile of rubble. My eyes searched, but I found nothing. No hint that she'd been here. No scrap of clothing. No bedding or mosquito netting. I could explain it all in my head. The storm damage. The gale force wind. The heavy rain, but nothing remained. I walked up to the tree.

"You want to believe she was real, and so she was." Colton paused behind me. "But only to you."

My hand fell heavily on the thick trunk and my head came forward. *I didn't dream her*, I told myself. I couldn't have. She was real. I felt her. I looked down at my hand, the hand that cupped her jaw and touched her body. The hand that held her to my chest and led her in a dance. The hand that covered hers as she stroked me and fingered her as I filled her. She was real.

I thought I heard my name, a shriek in the wind, but when I turned to Colton for confirmation he heard it, his expression hinted at nothing, and I dismissed the sound as the screech of a returning seagull. I felt for the small knife in my cargo short pocket and pulled it out. J M, I etched into the soft trunk of the tree and then added my initials under them. J.M. + T.C. She ruled over me. It was juvenile and crush-worthy, but it signified I'd been there. And so had she.

# 31

# Day 69 – Juliet

"Juliet," Lillian exhaled like a relieved mother. She pulled me to her and kissed my cheek. Pressing me back almost as quickly, she assessed my body, and I worried she could see the pleasure he'd given me.

"What happened to your head?" Her tone shifted, a soft shriek added to her concern. Nimble fingers touched over the scab.

"Oh, I was hit by a tree going up the mountain."

"You went up the mountain in that storm?" she questioned, looking past me. She'd found me a little distance from the tree house and I was eager to return to my things. My notes were safely tucked into my satchel but I had other valuables I wanted to check on. And then, I wanted to find Tack.

"There is a cave on higher ground, and we went there."

"We?" Lillian didn't even blink at the word. Her eyes widened, and her fingers dug into my arms.

"Yes. Lillian, I have so much to tell you," I chattered, attempting to step around her. A false smile formed on her face and her mouth twitched. "There's this—"

"You can tell me all about it on the boat," she said, interrupting me as she slipped her arm through mine and led me away from the island home.

"What?" I questioned, walking a few feet with her before tugging on her arm to stop us. "What boat?"

"Juliet, we haven't much time. You just lived through a hurricane, but another one is coming. We've come to bring you home."

"Home," I mouthed, the word nothing more than a whisper. I blinked back the sudden tears. I didn't have a home. I didn't want to leave. I had nowhere to go. I wanted Tack. "But I didn't finish my time.

The experiment. It isn't complete." I straightened, prepared to stand my ground and refuse to leave.

"The experiment is over. We cannot risk your life. We'll take the information you have, and you can complete the restoration in another manner on the mainland."

"But I…I can't leave Tack."

"Tack," she whispered, looking away from me for a moment. The false smile was back. "Why don't you tell me all about this Tack on the boat?" She reached for my arm, but I pulled back.

"No, I can't go without him. He was just behind me." I motioned over my shoulder, spinning in the direction to follow him. Lillian reached for me, gripping my wrist in a hold stronger than I could have imagined from her frame.

"As it appears, he's left you," she implied by looking around me, her head tilting from one side of my body to the other. "Perhaps you could explain him. On the boat." Her voice deepened as she spoke through her teeth.

"He…he didn't leave me. We…" My voice faded. A shaky hand came to my head. This was the very reason I hadn't mentioned him before, I told myself. Lillian wouldn't have understood. Plus, it would have ruined the experiment. Self-reflection. Isolated surroundings. Finding forgiveness. The last idea gave me pause. I didn't think I could forgive if I hadn't actually gotten to know Tack, learn who he was, who he *is*.

"Juliet, we are leaving for the boat. Now." Her tone broke my thoughts. Through clenched teeth, she smiled falsely once again. Her free hand balled into a fist. "It's either come with us or die. We won't be back." Her words startled me, the intention definite. Lillian wasn't giving me a choice. But how could I leave Tack behind?

"Let me show you where he is," I offered, but she snapped her fingers. Suddenly, I was hitched into the air over the shoulder of Franco. I hadn't heard him approach in the brush.

"Lillian," I begged, hoping my plea would stop her brisk stomp to the cove. My head riddled with confusion. Why was she doing this?

Where was Tack? What was happening? "Lillian, please." She ignored me as I jostled over Franco's shoulder.

"Tack!" I screamed, slowly beating on Franco's large back to no avail.

*Tack*, I whispered in my head. We hadn't passed the tree house. Instead, we traveled a short distance in the opposite direction before my feet were returned to the ground. All my thoughts told me to run to Tack as they hit the dock, but my feet took me forward as Lillian waited at the end. My legs felt thick like the tree trunks and I struggled with each step away from my familiar space on the island. I bit my lip, annoyed with myself for letting the reality of Tack escape. The heaviness of my body slowed me down and I suddenly felt sluggish like I hadn't slept in days.

"Look, we can pass the beach. It will prove no one is there."

Lightened by her words, the weight slowly slipped away as I followed behind her. The skiff I arrived in had been upgraded to an ocean-worthy speedboat. The size alone proved Lillian's fear of another hurricane. When the engine roared to life, it confirmed we were racing the weather.

We pulled out to the main water faster than I expected and veered left away from Tack's beach. A thought occurred to me.

"I never said the beach," I yelled over the roar of the motor, staring at Lillian as the boat shifted in the opposite direction of where I hoped we were headed.

"What?" she shouted in return.

"The beach. I never said he was at the beach." My eyes narrowed. "Why would you suggest we pass it unless you knew he was there?" I paused. "Did you know he'd be on the island?"

# 32
## The Island Tastes Your Loss

Juliet Montmore had nothing. While it had all been stripped away in one fateful night, it had been restored by another. He had given her everything for the briefest of moments. And then he was gone.

She stared at the departing island, knowing high above the shore there was a cave, and a storm, and a man. While she once thought this island meant freedom, she now felt more confined than ever—and betrayed. But she had no one to blame. She'd committed a crime after an act done to her. She'd put herself in the position to go to the island.

*Experiment*, she thought. She allowed herself to be part of the scientific process, and she felt played when she swore she'd never be taken advantage of again. She closed her eyes to the bite of the ocean spray, the salty air mixing with the struggling tears

*Repent.* The word drifted through her head. Without him, she wouldn't have been on this island. Without him, she wouldn't have found herself again. She offered forgiveness in exchange for love. She'd given him all of her. He took what he intended before they knew one another and then she gave it to him willingly. Because he asked. He wanted permission and she agreed—love him and be free.

*You make me wild*, he said, when all she wanted was to be cared for, cared about. She wanted to be claimed.

*Restore*, the liaison had said, but she'd never felt so broken. The further they sped from the island, the heavier her heart weighed in her chest. While she promised not to look back, she couldn't look away. She didn't want regrets. She wanted Tack. But she sensed he wasn't coming back, and he wasn't following her.

Her nose ran, and she reached for her satchel. Blindly, she stuck her hand in the bag and pulled out something unexpected. She pulled the book to her chest and turned back toward the island.

*You are going to cry*, the little prince said, or something like that, she recalled as her thumb stroked the back of the book. The little prince wondered how taming the fox had been for any good if the fox was going to cry when they departed. Slowly, she smiled with the thought. She knew their time on the island would come to an end at some point. It was sooner than expected, but she had gotten what she came for.

Through the tears, she smiled. Being tamed by him had done her all the good.

++

Terence Jackson Corbin IV understood right from wrong. He'd been doing wrong his whole life until he finally got it right. And then she got away. While he thought he wanted reckless and meaningless and bad, he'd learned that good and meaningful and fearless had been better. He'd been afraid, that's what he learned—afraid to love. Mainly because he didn't know how. Everything in his life had come easily to him, but love had not.

He might have lost his chance, had he not come to the island, and as the salty air whipped at his face and the sorrow filled his lungs, he realized the island had been what he was missing in life. And now, he was missing her. She'd disappeared.

He thought of her as she stood in that pond, staring up at him, vulnerable, frightened, but determined to stand her ground. A mouse. His mouse. He'd learned from the animal like Garvey had encouraged. He'd given to her what he wanted in return. He cared for her, cared *about* her—he loved her. And she was gone.

He stood with his knees pressed to the board at the stern of the boat. His hands in his pockets, he glanced down at his arm. There, resting on his left wrist, was the only evidence that she existed. He pulled his hand from the pocket and with his other hand he tugged at the bracelet. His frustration built, and he recognized the anger under his skin. *How could she leave him?* he thought as he struggled to remove the leaf-made jewelry. He planned to throw it in the ocean like some damn movie. *Take back your gift,* he cursed, but his eyes rose to the island, shaped like the curve of a woman jutting up from the water.

*How had he not seen it before?* She was the island. She was *his* island, and he knew he could not exist until he found her again. While his time on the land might be over, his redemption was not complete. He had her forgiveness. He had her love. But he needed *her* to make his circle complete.

*One year*, they had said, but an expiration could not be placed on what he discovered. With each mile he sped away from the island, the old Tack slowly returned. Powerful. Determined. Cunning. That's what he'd learned from her. He would have her.

*I will find you*, she'd said as parting words to him.

*Don't worry, Mouse*, he thought. *I will be looking for you.*

The story continues – <u>Return to the Island</u>

# Thank you

This story came on like a storm. For one solid month, I wrote, averaging anywhere from 6,000-10,000 words a day. Any author will tell you that's insane, and that's how this story felt. It consumed me. The idea of redemption, forgiveness, and love was so strong, it crept through my bones. I lived for these characters. And I hope you are living for them now as well.

Huge thank you to Shannon for another amazing cover and the patience of a saint as I went back and forth in my decision. Thank you again and again to my editor, Kiezha, for additional words of wisdom. Extra hugs to Molly McLain (USA Today Bestselling author of *Can't Shake You*) for your additional eyes, your inspiring words, and your tender support. More love to Karen for her eagle eyes at proofreading and Lisa for another set. Much love and laughs to my reader group, Loving L.B., for hanging out day in and day out.

Extra love always to my family. Thankfully, this was written in the summertime and MD, MK, JR and A were all at work while I wrote my days away. This meant dinner was only late a few times. More hugs to Mr. Dunbar, who lets me do my thing.

Again, I hope you've enjoyed Tack and Juliet's story. Tune in for more, and in the meantime, keep in touch...

## Connect with L.B. Dunbar

Stalk me: www.facebook.com/lbdunbarauthor
Search me: www.lbdunbar.com
Pin me: www.pinterest.com/lbdunbar/
Read me: www.goodreads.com/author/show/8195738.L_B_Dunbar
News about me: https://app.mailerlite.com/webforms/landing/j7j2s0
Hang with me: www.facebook.com/groups/LovingLB/
Tweet me: @lbdunbarwrites
Insta- me: @lbdunbarwrites

# Other Works by L.B. Dunbar

## The Sensations Collection
Small town, sweet and sexy stories of family and love.
*Sound Advice*
*Taste Test*
*Fragrance Free*
*Touch Screen*
*Sight Words*

## The Legendary Rock Star Series
Rock star mayhem in the tradition of King Arthur.
A classic tale with a modern twist of romance and suspense.
*The Legend of Arturo King*
*The Story of Lansing Lotte*
*The Quest of Perkins Vale*
*The Truth of Tristan Lyons*
*The Trials of Guinevere DeGrance*

## Paradise Stories
MMA chaos of biblical proportion between two brothers and
the fight for love.
*Paradise Tempted: The Beginning*
*Paradise Fought: Abel*
*Paradise Found: Cain*

## Stand Alones
*The Sex Education of M.E.*
*The History in Us*

## The Island Duet
*Redemption Island*
*Return to the Island*

## Modern Descendants – writing as elda lore
Hades
Solis
Heph

# About the Author

L.B. Dunbar loves the sweeter things in life: cookies, Coca-Cola, and romance. Her reading journey began with a deep love of fairy tales, medieval knights, Regency debauchery, and alpha males. She loves a deep belly laugh and a strong hug. Occasionally, she has the energy of a Jack Russell terrier. Accused—yes, that's the correct word—of having an over active imagination, to her benefit, such an imagination works well. Author of over a dozen novels, she's created sweet, small town worlds; rock star mayhem; MMA chaos; sexy rom-coms for the over 40; and suspense on an island of redemption. In addition, she is earning a title as the "myth and legend lady" for her modernizations of mythology as elda lore. Her other duties in life include mother to four children and wife to the one and only.

78409632R00090

Made in the USA
Lexington, KY
08 January 2018